The Seven *of* Senses *Italy*

la luna di miele

Nicole Gregory

THE
MENTORIS
PROJECT

The Mentoris Project
745 Sierra Madre Boulevard
San Marino, CA 91108

Copyright © 2022 The Mentoris Project

Cover image from Shutterstock.com
Map by Free Vector Maps / http://freevectormaps.com

More information at www.mentorisproject.org

ISBN: 978-1-947431-53-9

Library of Congress Control Number: 2022947140

Publisher's Cataloging-in-Publication (Provided by Cassidy Cataloguing Services, Inc.)

Names: Gregory, Nicole, 1953- author.
Title: The seven senses of Italy : la luna di miele / Nicole Gregory.
Description: San Marino, CA : The Mentoris Project, [2022]
Identifiers: ISBN: 978-1-947431-53-9 (paperback) | 9798215907955 (ebook) | LCCN: 2022947140
Subjects: LCSH: Newlyweds--Fiction. | Honeymoons--Italy--Fiction. | Italy--Description and travel-- Fiction. | Americans--Italy--Fiction. | Romance fiction, American. | LCGFT: Romance fiction. | Travel writing. | BISAC: FICTION / Romance / Holiday. | FICTION / Romance / Clean & Wholesome. | TRAVEL / Europe / Italy. | FICTION / Romance / Contemporary.
Classification: LCC: PS3607.R489 S48 2022 | DDC: 813/.6--dc23

Contents

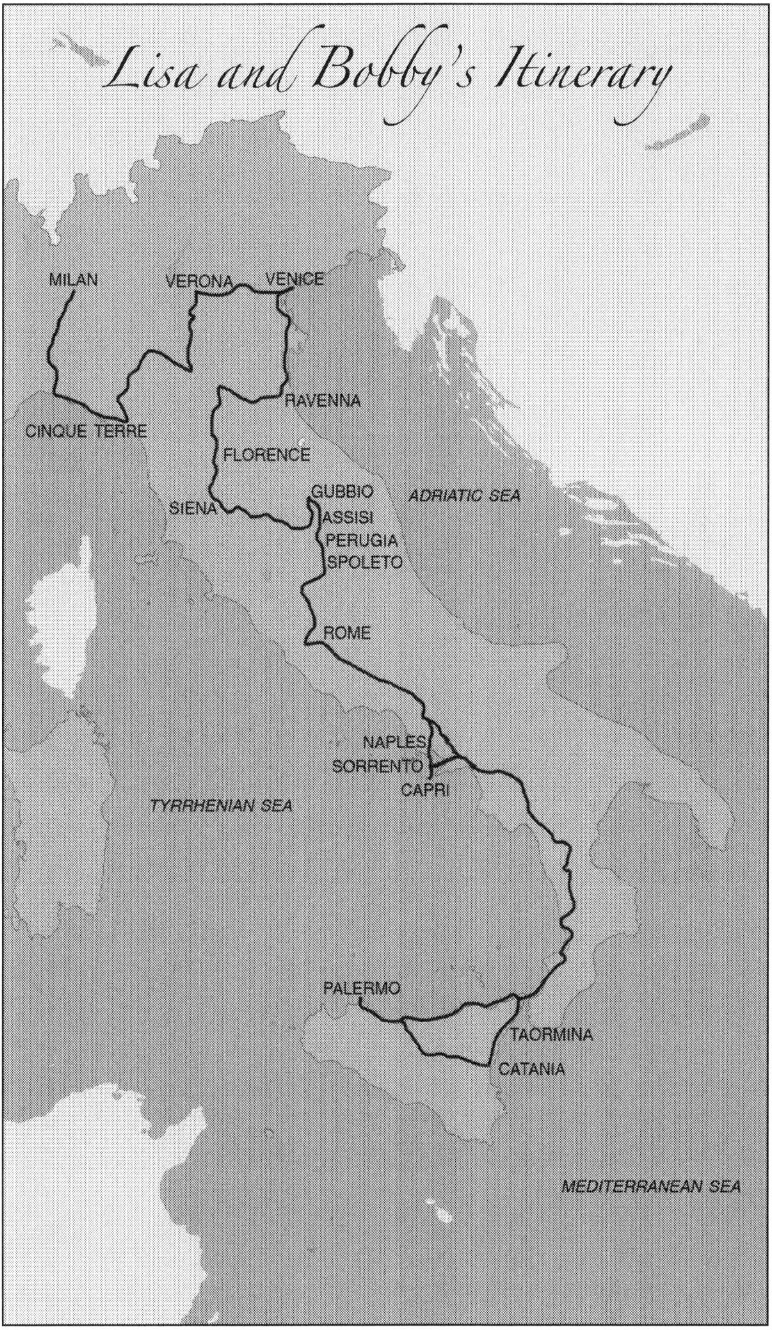
Lisa and Bobby's Itinerary
MILAN
VERONA
VENICE
RAVENNA
CINQUE TERRE
FLORENCE
GUBBIO
ADRIATIC SEA
SIENA
ASSISI
PERUGIA
SPOLETO
ROME
NAPLES
SORRENTO
CAPRI
TYRRHENIAN SEA
PALERMO
TAORMINA
CATANIA
MEDITERRANEAN SEA

Introduction

Dear reader, let me introduce myself.

Sono io, Nina, *la nonna di* Lisa.

I am long gone from this earthly world. But from my heavenly view, I keep watch over my family. I am hovering over my beautiful granddaughter Lisa and I see she has found a nice young man—this makes me happy. I watched her grow up when I came to America to live with my daughter, Lisa's mamma, and her family. Little Lisa and I, we loved each other very much, until, well, my time on Earth came to an end. I showed her how to grow herbs in our backyard, how to pick the ripest tomatoes for the finest sauce.

I want Lisa and her boyfriend to see my country—some people call it the Old Country, but it is old *and* new. If I can pull the strings of fate just a little, they will soon be on their way to Italy to see all its beautiful treasures. I will watch over them, and maybe push a little in this or that direction all during their adventure. Of course, they will not know I am watching, guiding, but that is as it should be, eh?

Another thing—*per favore*, I have asked this writer to help me describe Italy—you know, there is so much beauty, history . . . so many stories and people who changed the world. I hope you don't mind. She will help me explain why we Italians are so good at what we do. I don't mean only the famous ones—Leonardo da Vinci, Sophia Loren, Luciano Pavarotti—but a nonna like me: women who feed their families every day, the people who go to work, sweep the streets, teach the children, the ones nobody writes about. You'll see.

Now I pray that Lisa and Bobby—and you too, dear reader—keep hearts and minds open to all of Italy's treasures, some in plain sight, some hidden.

Watch with me—these two, they are in love!

BROOKLYN, NEW YORK

Bobby is uncharacteristically quiet. Lisa notices it immediately when she meets him to walk along the promenade in

Brooklyn before going out to dinner. He is slightly agitated, even though it is Friday, the end of the workweek.

The city glitters majestically across the water in the twilight of the autumn day. Lisa happily rattles on about her graduate studies in resilience as they walk. She loves her work, but it is challenging. Tall, with dark eyes and curly brown hair, Bobby listens attentively. Lisa and Bobby have been together for two years and feel completely at ease with one another. So obviously in love, the couple attracts the notice of passersby.

"I just want to start interviewing real people rather than just studying theory," she complains. "I want to find out what really makes people resilient, why some survive and thrive and others don't. And I have to identify my thesis topic by the end of the year."

Bobby takes Lisa's hand affectionately. "Lisa," he says, slowing his pace. Then he stops and looks at her. "Lisa . . ."

Now she stares at him intently. *Is something wrong?* she wonders.

Suddenly, he kneels in front of her and all agitation vanishes from his face. "Will you marry me? Will you be my wife?" His voice is calm and even, and his dark eyes look directly at hers.

"What? I . . . yes! Yes! Oh, gosh, Bobby!" She throws her arms around him as he stands up. Passersby observing the scene start to clap. Bobby brings a box out of his pocket and opens it—inside is a thin gold ring with a diamond that catches the light of the streetlamp. He gently puts it on Lisa's finger. Both their hands tremble.

"Well, now, I guess we are engaged!" He laughs and hugs Lisa. Happy tears form in her eyes. "We will have a life of joy, love, beauty, and adventure. I want us to try new things together, learn together."

"We must go to Italy for our honeymoon," Lisa says with a smile. "My nonna Nina—she always wanted me to see Italy. She grew up in Sicily. I have a cousin there I haven't seen in years . . . her name is Lucia."

"Excellent idea," Bobby says. "And we can visit our friend from college, Marco—he's in Sicily now."

"We can see Rome and Florence and Venice," Lisa says.

"And swim at those beautiful beaches."

"And eat amazing food and drink incredible wine!" Lisa stops and smiles. "But first, we have the small matter of a wedding to plan."

"And right now we need to eat dinner." Bobby puts his arm around Lisa and leads her down the cobblestone street to their favorite Italian restaurant.

MILAN (six months later)

The small hotel room is filled with morning sunlight. Red geraniums on the window stand out against the blue sky above. Bobby and Lisa are jet-lagged, exhausted, and still reeling from their wedding in the US. Slowly, they wake and open their eyes on the first morning of their honeymoon in Italy.

"*Milano*," Bobby says, looking up at the small chandelier dangling from the high ceiling. "I will never say 'Milan' again, because the locals call this city *Milano*—accent on the N."

Lisa smiles. "As you wish. I just can't believe we're here. I'm so excited!" She hops out of bed to open the windows.

"Lisa, there is one thing you might not know about me—I wander," Bobby intones with mock seriousness.

"What do you mean, wander?" she asks.

"I like to walk with no guidebook—no guidebook written for foreign tourists, that is. I know you are a fast-moving woman, with places to go and people to see. But I want to go slow sometimes so we can get to know this country. In fact, while we are here, I don't want to take a taxi or bus—ever!"

"What about a romantic gondola ride?" Lisa asks.

"Oh, yes, a gondola." *How lucky I am*, he thinks, smiling. *I've married a smart, beautiful woman with a sense of humor.*

Bobby is an architect, just beginning his career. Before he and Lisa left the US, he had applied for his dream job at a small firm. He was glad to let Italy distract him from his underlying anxiety: Would he get that job?

"I *will* bring the guidebook," Lisa says, running a brush through her long red-brown hair. She has wanted to visit Italy for years to understand her grandmother, and even herself, better. She's looked forward to seeing her cousin again too—as an only child, Lisa has always longed to have a big Italian family.

In her study of resilience, she recalls stories about how

her nonna grew food for her family and then left Italy when her husband died. It seems to Lisa that her nonna was incredibly resilient—Lisa wants to understand where that resilience came from.

Bobby is intent on seeing all the city's architecture and its art—but Lisa's mission is to discover the inner lives of Italians. Suddenly, she sees a symmetry: He wants to understand the *external* expressions of Italian sensibility and she is fascinated by their *internal* workings.

"Wandering is fine," she says, "but I don't want to miss places like the Leonardo da Vinci Museum in Florence—it has all his designs for helicopters and submarines . . ."

"Yes, of course, we have to see that. But do you mind if we wander a bit every day? Put away the see-every-famous-sight list and just see what we see?"

Lisa nods silently. She has just noticed the outfit Bobby has chosen for the day: faded shorts and a T-shirt. His curly dark hair is barely combed. She adores her new husband, but . . . those clothes? *How can I convince him to dress a little better?*

Soon the newlyweds are strolling along the cobblestone streets of Milan. Lisa is short, Bobby is tall, yet they saunter comfortably with each other. A sight up ahead makes them both smile: a sign for a *caffé* bar. They follow their noses to the source of freshly made espresso.

"*Buongiorno*," the barista welcomes them with a friendly smile.

"*Per favore, espresso—due. Grazie*," Bobby says, pleased

he memorized this phrase from his Italian language book that morning.

But the barista replies to him in English. "Of course. Are you on vacation? Did you just arrive?"

"Yes—*sì!*" Lisa says. Was it so obvious they are sleep-deprived Americans? "We just got here last night."

"Ah, very good!" the barista says cheerfully while preparing their coffee.

Bobby turns to Lisa. "You know, Milano is the banking capital of Italy."

"I thought it was the *fashion* capital of the *world*."

"Aha! Sounds like shopping is in your future," Bobby says with a smile.

As the barista brings their tiny espresso cups, Lisa asks, "*Per favore*, what do you suggest we see on our first day here?"

"There is plenty to see in Milano, old and new, all within walking distance," the young woman replies. "You must visit the Duomo—the *cattedrale*—you can go to the top and see all of the city. And then you must walk along the Naviglio Grande, the canal. And you must go to Galleria Vittorio Emanuele for shopping."

"Oh, I want to go there!" Lisa says.

"I recommend you just start walking," the barista says. "Put away your map for now. You don't need it. Have your *caffè*, then let your eyes, ears, and nose take you on an adventure."

Bobby throws a satisfied glance at Lisa.

"Okay, you win—for now," Lisa says to him. After paying,

now charged up with strong Italian coffee, the couple heads out.

"Ciao!" the barista calls out after them.

Stepping out into the sunshine, Lisa says, "I love the word *ciao*. It's just so happy."

She and Bobby stare, utterly fascinated by the scene: Milanese people walking quickly to work, shop owners getting ready for customers, cars and scooters pushing their way down the street. A child trudges past, carrying a heavy backpack—she calls out to her mother ahead and runs to catch up with her. A bus lumbers by. A man carrying a basket of flowers strides past, wafting a sweet floral fragrance in his wake. A church bell rings in the distance.

They turn to look at each other and laugh. "Which way," Lisa asks, "left or right?"

"Well . . . let's turn right!" And their adventure begins.

Within minutes they come upon an open piazza next to a basilica.

"What is this?" Lisa asks. They halt and turn around, taking in the old brick structure, before Lisa leads them inside.

Bobby has to walk fast to keep up with her. They enter the basilica's courtyard, then find their way into the church itself. Flickering votive candles sit on top of long rectangular tables along the sides and the red and white archways of the church ceiling separate the structural sections.

"It's the Basilica of Saint Ambrose," Bobby whispers, staring at a bronze plaque explaining the building's history. He gazes up at the frescoes on the walls that depict the life of the saint.

"I know from my Italian architecture class that part of it was designed by Donato Bramante—he also worked on the design for Saint Peter's in Rome."

"Wow, how do you remember these details?" Lisa whispers back.

Bobby smiles. "I just like history—especially when it comes to art and architecture. It's the story of our past."

They quietly step forward to better hear the angelic voices of a small choir. A service is taking place, and everyone is respectfully silent, even turning off their phones. Some people sit, eyes closed, in the dark wooden pews.

"Saint Ambrose—he's the patron saint of Milan," Lisa says under her breath. "He was the bishop of Milan, and in fact, he is the one who baptized Saint Augustine." She pauses, thinking back to the lessons about him from her nonna and Catholic school. "I think he's the one who didn't even want to be bishop, but everyone who met him knew he was right for the job. He gave away almost all his land and belongings when he became bishop and that made people love him even more."

"Saint Augustine's famous line is, 'Grant me continence and chastity, but not yet,'" Bobby says. "I guess he admired virtue in theory, but he was not ready to give up his concubine." They laugh quietly.

"I can see why Ambrose liked Augustine—they both understood human weaknesses," Lisa says thoughtfully.

"Does Ambrose have a feast day?" Bobby asks. His wife is an expert on the saints and knows their feast days. *His wife!* The word sounds strange and wonderful.

"December seventh," she answers, giving him a look that says, *Doesn't everyone know that?*

Bobby considers an idea: *Maybe a happy marriage doesn't happen when two people are alike, but when they perfectly complement each other.* He doesn't have to know the feast days, because Lisa does.

And she doesn't have to know the names of the architects who designed Italian cathedrals, because he has that covered.

The Sensual Nature of Italy

No country thrills and delights the senses quite like Italy.

The sense of taste, for instance—one of life's great sensuous pleasures—is brought to new heights by Italian food. From Italy's north to the south, food is a gift of love and friendship, deeply gratifying for the cook and greatly appreciated by the eater.

Or the sense of hearing, for which beautiful music is created. Music is simply part of Italian life and expression. Remember how Italians responded to quarantines during the coronavirus pandemic? Spontaneously, they went to their balconies to sing together, boosting morale for the whole world. They instinctively knew music unifies people, lifting their spirits and hearts. At one point in history, an act from Verdi's opera *Nabucco* was sung as a kind of patriotic anthem. Hearing music, making music, singing—these are essential Italian experiences.

Italians appreciate the sensuous—the warmth of the seaside sun or the heat of a natural thermal spring. They like the look and the feel of fine, well-made fabrics. They are famous for dressing well.

As soon as visitors arrive in Italy, a certain seduction begins. They feel their muscles relax in the warm climate. They sigh with the first tastes of flavorful food, the first sips of rich wine. They gaze at the stunning art, moved by its mystery and beauty. And they are drawn to the lifestyle that puts simple human pleasures first.

La dolce vita.

Their values and priorities reorder. Writers who've fallen in love with Italy articulate clearly this life-changing effect. One is Frances Mayes, who wrote about it in her memoir *Under the Tuscan Sun*. Her book touched a nerve, becoming a bestseller that sold millions of copies in multiple languages

Dear reader, *sono io*, Nina. I am whispering into the souls of Lisa and Bobby, telling them to be open to all Italy offers. Let's see what happens . . . I have seen my country's magic touch the hearts of people, and now I hope it touches theirs.

With the senses, *prendere nota*—take notice!

When Italians tell you stories, listen—they know a few things. Waiters, shopkeepers, bus drivers, and train conductors will all open whole worlds for you if you take time to listen. My papà, a farmer, would take vegetables and herbs into our town to sell, but what he liked best was talking to his friends—the other farmers, the village women who bought from him, the children wandering through the piazza, all of them.

And if he came upon a stranger—lucky for them! My papà would begin his long stories about the village, how the river once overflowed and flooded the streets, how lightning once struck a pig far on the edge of town and sent the other pigs running in every direction. He knew all the families who lived there—he knew their good fortune, their unlucky times. He wanted everyone to know how beautiful that place was, so he would ask visitors if they had seen the church yet. I went to church every Sunday, of course—everyone did!

I wish Papà were still living in the world with my Lisa and Bobby. He could teach these young ones a thing or two about being a good person; about sharing what you have but getting a good price for what you sell; about taking care of your family, your children; about looking at people in the eye.

Italians are very friendly—*amichevoli*. Watch how they go about their day, how they greet each other in passing, how an old man lingers on the street to chat with friends.

I urge Lisa and Bobby to allow Italy's warm welcome to pour into their souls.

Sight

TREASURES FOR THE EYES

CINQUE TERRE

"Oh, my gosh!" Lisa gasps at the fairy tale–like scene before her. "It's so . . . pretty!" But "pretty" hardly describes the colorful view of buildings and rocks and ocean.

The tiny seaside village of Vernazza, awash in glorious summer light, spreads out before her from the high, rocky promontory where she and Bobby have stopped. The village appears as if from a child's dream: the colorful boxy houses perch around a harbor like birds on a fountain. At the water's edge, long boats and wide bistro umbrellas dot the scene. The broad blue sea stretches out to infinity.

The two have been hiking through Cinque Terre in the region of Liguria. They arrived having driven from Milan the day before in a rented car.

It's hot, and to catch his sweat, Bobby has wrapped a red bandanna around his head. Lisa is glad she packed a wide-brimmed straw hat. The bright sun beats down and the trails force them to climb steep hill after steep hill. The hardy hikers' reward is a succession of spectacular views of the charming villages and the rugged, irregular coastline. Other hikers are also enjoying the trails today—too many for Bobby.

"Let's go down there and find lunch," Lisa says, and Bobby enthusiastically nods his head. They begin the descent into Vernazza.

Soon they are happily seated at a table in Piazza Marconi next to the water. While they wait for their food, Bobby pulls a book from his daypack and reads about Vernazza. Lisa stares at the passing people, the steep hills dotted with little houses, and the glittering sea, while appreciating the glass of white wine the waiter delivered promptly. *My legs are going to be sore from all this hiking—but it's worth it*, she thinks.

Surrounded by natural and man-made beauty, Bobby and Lisa scan the intensely picturesque spot. Cinque Terre—or five small towns—along the Italian Riviera are connected by walkable coastal paths. The hills were made into steep terraces that dip toward the sea. For hundreds of years, residents of the ancient towns have tended crops and vineyards on these terraced hills. In 1997, Cinque Terre was named a UNESCO World Heritage Site in recognition of the unique beauty and geography of its villages.

"I could die now—this has to be one of the most beautiful

places on Earth," Lisa says as she lifts her face to the warm sun and stretches out her arms as if to welcome it all.

Over time, the vineyards of Cinque Terre became increasingly difficult to maintain and some of the famed stone buttresses collapsed due to lack of care. The Italian Ministry of the Environment stepped up to help preserve the towns, in a unified effort with the World Monuments Watch and funding from American Express. By conducting architectural surveys and training local researchers, they created a plan for sustainable development.

"I like that the towns can be reached by ferry or train—but not cars," Lisa reflects. "And it's amazing that these villages sit on top of cliffs and promontories. Each town looks like it is the home of princesses and princes."

"Let's review all the towns," Bobby says. "Monterosso is where we started, of course—it has the long beach and medieval center."

"We deserve a medal for the hike here from Monterosso!" Lisa says.

"It should get easier as we hike down the coast," Bobby says, examining a map.

"We must visit the Doria Castle while we are here in Vernazza," Lisa says. "It juts right out into the sea."

"Okay, and next we will hike to Corniglia," Bobby says. "It looks like an amazing, beautiful town perched high above the sea. Then we will keep going to Manarola, and finally Riomaggiore, which has a fishing village, vineyards, and a thirteenth-century castle that overlooks the sea."

"And how many hours will this take?" Lisa asks, tilting her head skeptically.

The waiter appears carrying two plates of spaghetti with clams, shrimp, and mussels, and places them down carefully—so Bobby doesn't answer the question. They dig in hungrily.

"The charm of these villages," Lisa says, taking a sip of chilled wine, "is that they are small, built to a human scale around the promontories of the coast."

"It's the whole scene," Bobby adds. "Ancient churches and castles . . . homes painted in all different colors . . . and with the blue ocean in the background." He looks at his map again, then adds, "This will probably take us another four to five hours."

"Ohhh, I hope my legs can do this!" Lisa says.

VERONA

Dear reader, do you see what I mean? Yes, I have been to these little towns before, a long time ago, when my legs were strong and I could hike any hill or mountain!

In my country, in these little towns, I see my people. I am from Sicily, but still, in little towns are families that are knit together because they share the market, the church, the schools, and their histories. Their children grow up together, and they help each other.

When I was young, families stayed together—do you understand? Everyone knew each other for years and years. We didn't leave, or most of us did not; we stayed with our families.

But now I see Lisa and Bobby are resting from their hiking. You watch—by tomorrow, they will be completely revived. Myself? I would need a week . . . my old joints are resting fine here in heaven.

That night, Bobby and Lisa recuperate at their hotel restaurant, relishing the triumph of having hiked through Cinque Terre, even though their muscles ache. After a delicious dinner, they sit back at their outdoor table to enjoy a coffee. Tourists stream by, wide-eyed and happy.

"Lots of tourists here," Lisa says. "It's amazing Italy can accommodate so many of them."

"I read there are about thirty-two thousand hotels—large and small—in Italy," Bobby says. "They do a good business!" Too fatigued and full of good food for an after-dinner walk, they head back to the hotel.

Bright and early the next morning, the couple rents a tiny car to drive to Verona. It's going to be an incredible night. Months earlier, Bobby bought tickets to *Aida*, which is being performed at the Verona Arena, about a three-hour drive away.

But the drive there proves to be harder than he figures—the road signs are utterly confusing.

He grips the wheel of the rented Alfa Romeo. "Why didn't I learn more Italian?" he shouts when he misses the turnoff he wanted for the third time.

"Don't worry, it's okay to get lost, remember?" Lisa laughs, then sits up straight and pushes her hair out of her eyes. "Go that way!" she shouts. Bobby makes an abrupt sharp turn, wheels squealing, and within minutes they spot Verona.

Located in the Veneto region, Verona's population is about 250,000 people. It's known to most people as the setting for several of Shakespeare's plays, including *Two Gentlemen of Verona* and *Romeo and Juliet*. Though *Romeo and Juliet* is fictional, the fourteenth-century Casa di Giulietta was supposedly the home of the Capulets. A steady stream of tourists visits the casa and a statue of Juliet nearby.

After finding their hotel in Verona, Bobby and Lisa—their legs now accustomed to walking hours each day—pick up their daypacks and set off on foot to explore the city. They are intrigued by ancient rose-colored buildings and the slow-moving Adige River.

"*AH-deejeh*," Bobby says, practicing the correct pronunciation.

That evening they are eager for the big event of their Verona visit. They walk to the Verona Arena, a large and impeccably restored ancient stone structure. A crowd of well-dressed opera lovers gathers near the entrance, humming with excitement.

They pass through the entrance and Bobby clambers up the steep stone steps with Lisa close behind. He notices everyone makes way for the older adults, patiently waiting as they slowly climb the steps. They find their seats and, along with thousands of others in the arena, they eagerly anticipate the performance. As the sun sets, a large, bright full moon rises in the darkening sky. Lights on the perimeter create a magical atmosphere.

"This arena used to hold thirty thousand people," Bobby says in a hushed voice. "Now they let in only about fifteen thousand."

Ushers hand out small candles to the audience, and one by one, each person shares the light with the next in their row. Lisa turns to two older women next to her to light their candles, then she and Bobby follow the lead of everyone else: they hold theirs aloft. The sight of thousands of dots of shimmering candles cascading down the rows of the arena readies the audience for the magic of the epic story.

In a moment of absolute silence, the conductor raises his baton and the violins and orchestra suddenly begin. The stage lights up slowly on the magnificent set, and a collective gasp ripples through the crowd. Singers quietly file onto the stage and the performance begins to unfold.

At the first intermission, Lisa strikes up a conversation with the two women beside her. They are cousins who've traveled from Florence to see the performance.

"For us Italians, opera has personal meaning," explains the woman who introduces herself as Ariana.

"There is silly opera, and serious opera," chimes in her cousin, Antonia. "When you hear serious opera, the range of the human voice, it's magnificent. Did you ever hear Luciano Pavarotti? So handsome, so charismatic. His characterization of Radames was beautiful . . ."

"*La sua voce era bellissima.*"

"*Sì, sì,*" Ariana agrees, sadly shaking her head.

"His voice—I shall never forget that voice." The two cousins speak as if mourning the loss of a lover.

"He started a foundation, you know. It continues to help new young opera singers to this day," Ariana says. "He was very generous."

"That's wonderful," Bobby says.

"*Aida* was first performed in Egypt," Antonia says. "Not many people know this."

"Commissioned by an Egyptian sultan!" Ariana adds.

"She knows a lot of history," Antonia whispers to Bobby and Lisa, "but so do I—so I like to test her. What year was that?" she challenges.

"1873," Ariana says.

"*No, hai torto*—it was 1871!" Antonia corrects triumphantly.

"*Aida* was first performed in *this* arena in 1913 at the hundredth anniversary of the birthday of Verdi," Ariana says confidently. "Operas have been performed here ever since, with the exception of two periods during World War I and World War II."

"How interesting!" Lisa says with genuine appreciation. The air is chilly—she pulls her sweater over her shoulders. The whole place feels like another world, and these two cousins are like walking encyclopedias, telling its history.

"Oh, we could talk about opera all day and all night—we've been coming here for years," Ariana says. "You know, Verdi didn't like it when *Aida* was performed in Cairo, because only rich people were allowed to see it. So, when it was performed in Milano, at La Scala, to him that was the real first performance because it was open to everyone to see, rich and poor."

What a treasure trove of stories older people carry with them! Bobby thinks. He decides to take his cue from Italians and show senior citizens the respect they obviously deserve.

God willing, one day he and Lisa will be old too, and would wish for the same.

VENICE

Dear reader, what did I tell you, eh? To hear Aida in that ancient arena. *Mamma mia!* The opera is . . . *bella.* I have not been to that place, or to any opera theater, but my uncle Giuseppe, he liked to sing all the time. He sang at parties, while he worked, and even at funerals. He was a baker, a chef! Don't think he was always happy—he had trouble with his wife, as I remember. But he sang through it all. I grew up hearing that deep voice around our house, coming through the windows. But wait . . . where are our two lovebirds now? I've lost track of them!

Ah, there they are—the young newlyweds are seated on that sleek high-speed train. I don't understand this fast pace—those two are trying to see so much in so little time! I fear they are missing something, the simple everyday joys of my country.

But this is their first visit, and hopefully there will be many more.

Look, I see now that their train is pulling slowly into Stazione di Santa Lucia in Venezia, and they have just awakened from a pleasant nap in their seats . . .

Lisa shakes herself awake as the train jolts slightly and the conductor strides down the corridor. She is amazed how much of Italy can be traversed at high speed. The Italian rail network—about ten thousand miles of mostly electric lines—is a major modern achievement. During World War II, Italy's train lines were severely damaged, and rebuilt as soon as possible. Today, rail passengers can explore Italy via comfortable, high-speed trains between most of the country's main cities.

"*Venezia!*" the conductor's voice booms over the loud-speaker as passengers gather their belongings.

"I'm calling it *Venezia* from now on," Bobby says as he grabs his bag from above, and when it falls heavily into his arms he thinks, *Why, oh why, did I bring so many books?*

Before he can hoist the bag on his shoulder, Lisa has already pushed ahead to get off the train and onto the station platform. He rushes to catch up. They leave the station together and are immediately confronted with a lively crowd of people streaming along on the wide waterside street named Fondamenta Santa Lucia. Warm, hazy sunlight fills the atmosphere.

Such a rich scene! Lisa's eyes latch onto a quick-moving vaporetto—or water bus—sleek black gondolas, and small motorboats as they course along the sparkling Grand Canal.

Bobby's heart jumps at the sight of the San Simeone Piccolo across the water, a commanding eighteenth-century church with long steps, a massive green dome, and a temple-like entrance supported by Corinthian columns. *I've got that church in my books!* he thinks. Next to it in line are the facades of more aging but elegant buildings, like a row of old friends on a bench.

Down a bit, the bridge called Ponte degli Scalzi crawls with crowds of tourists who drag their rolling suitcases first one way, then another, and finally stop to examine their maps.

"Oh. My. Goodness. This is beautiful," Bobby says reverently as he surveys the scene.

"Venice! I've seen hundreds of photos of this place . . . but to *be* here, surrounded by these pink, green, and orange buildings, and the canals. I can't believe it!" Lisa exclaims.

"The Accademia, the Peggy Guggenheim Collection, the Doge's Palace, the Correr Museum—all gold mines," Bobby muses. "And they're all here in this little city. I wonder how we can see them all."

"By walking from one to another," Lisa deadpans. "Unless we go by one of the boat taxis . . ."

"There is a lot of modern art here too," Bobby says. "Every other year, the Biennial, or *La Biennale di Venezia*, is held here."

"Okay," Lisa says urgently, "let's find our hotel so we can drop off our suitcases and start exploring this amazing place!"

They hurry along the crowded street, aromas of food, coffee, canal water, and strong cigarettes filling the air. Sunlight sparkles off the water and lively conversations of Italians and travelers surround them. They finally find the door of their small hotel and go inside to register.

"We must go to Piazza San Marco," Lisa says as she finishes unpacking in their little room with tall windows. "I know there is so much to see, but let's start there."

"Just to remind you, I hate tour groups," Bobby says, changing his shoes and socks. "I am preparing for major-league walking."

Minutes later, a block away from Saint Mark's Square, a voice echoes off the stone walls. "You are standing in the middle of San Marco, the famous Venice piazza!" shouts a young man leading a tour group of mostly older Americans who listen attentively.

Lisa and Bobby look at each other. Bobby starts to head in the opposite direction, but Lisa pulls on his sleeve. "Can't we just listen to a little of what he's explaining?"

"I told you, I do *not* like tours," Bobby says firmly. But, he admits, they could just listen in without having to actually join one. So, the two quietly step forward to hear the guide's words. The young man's dark hair is brushed straight back and he holds aloft a little orange flag so his group can find him. Lisa eyes his clothes. He wears a white shirt and clean, pressed jeans. *Very neat, and very Italian*, she thinks.

"Let's do a three-sixty turn and take in these facades and open spaces—they have been the same for hundreds of years," the guide says. He points up and the Americans' eyes follow. "First, you see here the magnificent Basilica di San Marco, or Saint Mark's Basilica. It is outrageously beautiful and colorful, don't you think? It features five entrance portals." The guide spins on his heels. "Keep turning, everyone—and now gaze upon the Palazzo Ducale, the Doge's Palace, an example of Gothic architecture that has survived fires and floods. It served as the doge's apartments and government offices at the end of the Piazzetta di San Marco—that long space—you can see the Grand Canal."

"I've seen photos of San Marco completely flooded," comments an American woman.

"Yes," the guide replies, "that does happen, and it is a constant worry because of the damage to the buildings."

Bobby looks around and wonders what it would be like to see this whole space under two feet of water. He shakes off the image, too terrible to contemplate.

"Now look up, *way* up," the guide says, "to the *Campanile di San Marco*, a three-hundred-twenty-three-foot-high brown brick bell tower." The tourists crane their necks all at once. "It has survived fires and earthquakes, and in 1902 it fell down. We rebuilt it ten years later—with a gilded angel on top. And now, keep turning!" he calls.

Everyone turns in their places, taking in the entire piazza scene with restaurants, bistros, and shops. "Come back in the evening and you will be treated to the sound of competing bands—they fill the air with wonderful music." The guide's obvious love for the place is infectious, and the Americans look around with interest.

As they cross the gray stones, Lisa and Bobby tag along behind. A flock of pigeons suddenly flies up and over them. A jazz band warms up on a platform stage. The dark waters of the Grand Canal ripple, and a statue of a bronze winged lion symbolizing Venice looks down on them from atop a column on the side of the square.

"Italians who live in and around this magnificent architecture—they like to party!" the young guide jokes. "The most famous party of all is the Carnival of Venice, which ends on Shrove Tuesday at the beginning of Lent. It was first celebrated in Venice in 1162 and began as a huge party where everyone wore elaborate masks, according to legend. The carnival was outlawed intermittently for many years but came back in 1979—which is right, for after all, it is a piece of Italian history."

"What's that over there?" asks a teenager in the group.

"In the corner sits Museo Correr. It's another former palace—it is full of preserved treasures," the guide replies. The group makes their way over to its entrance.

Lisa tugs on Bobby's sleeve. "I want to climb it," she says.

"Climb what?"

"The Campanile!" Lisa exclaims. "Let's go!"

Before Bobby can protest, Lisa pulls him along to the Campanile's entrance. She produces two tickets. *When did she buy those?* Bobby wonders.

Up they climb. Out of breath at the top of the great bell

tower, they scan the expanse before them. Below, Venice looks small and compact, like a jigsaw puzzle of rooftops—many with colorful gardens—and church towers and apartment houses with laundry hanging from clotheslines strung between windows.

Lisa sighs, scanning her eyes over the scene. "Venice is only two miles long," she says, "but so beautiful."

"So many islands surround Venice . . . Murano, Burano, Lido di Venezia . . ." Bobby says.

"San Servolo . . ." Lisa continues. "It's a tiny rectangular island that held the insane men and women of Venice for hundreds of years." At Bobby's surprised look, she says, "I know—it's hard to believe. I read about it in school. In the 1720s, insane men were sent there, and later in the century women were too. Almost no one ever came *out* of San Servolo. The asylum was run by a religious order and wasn't shut down until 1978. Now there is a museum to tell the story—and it's not a happy one."

"I think I'd rather visit Murano and Burano," Bobby says.

Lisa nods in agreement. They gaze out again at the view below. "I know every country has dark events in its past, and I don't want to ignore them," she says. "But right now, I want to dwell on the positives."

They climb down the tower, then meander through the streets of Venice, discovering pretty piazzas, crossing small bridges, and following crooked alleyways. Soon Lisa and Bobby begin to feel hungry. They agree to look for one restaurant recommended by a friend.

Already at ease in this ancient city, they find it strangely enjoyable not to know quite where they are. Venice is so small that getting lost is really impossible. The air cools and the afternoon sky settles into a soft gold-pink.

"Look!" Lisa says suddenly. Bobby follows her pointed finger across the water to a small church with its front doors flung open. Elegantly dressed men and women mingling on the terrace turn as a long wooden motorboat putters slowly down the canal toward the church.

Lisa gasps. Stepping out of the boat onto the little piazza is a slim young man wearing a tuxedo and a white rose pinned to his lapel. Lisa and Bobby recognize the man as a groom. And his bride is next to arrive. As the young man is hustled inside the church, another long boat pulls up to the landing. A tall young woman wearing a tight-fitting ivory gown steps out. Several older men hold her hands and lead her to solid ground. The family and friends in the wedding party gather in front of the church and file in for the ceremony.

Lisa and Bobby continue their walk, searching for the restaurant, getting hungrier by the minute. "I can't wait to try *bigoli*—Venice is famous for the thick pasta noodles," Lisa says.

"And I can't wait to try the seafood risotto," Bobby says.

At last, they spy their restaurant up ahead and hurry toward it.

They take their time over dinner, savoring the dimensions of flavor of the simple but delicious dishes. As they finish dessert, Lisa muses, "You know, I think seeing that happy wedding is a good sign for our trip."

She turns her head and listens, and then Bobby hears it too. Bells ring loudly, joyfully, somewhere nearby.

"The wedding—it must be over and now they are celebrating!" Bobby says, grabbing Lisa's hand. "I think it's a good sign for our marriage too—to experience this beautiful country together. Do you think it's too late for a gondola ride?"

After dinner they cross Piazza San Marco once again, this time toward a landing area where handsome young Italian gondoliers in striped shirts lounge, waiting for their next customers. They chat amiably with each other, looking as relaxed as they would be in their own living rooms.

Bobby reads the sign listing the fees and shakes his head at the cost for a ride. The gondoliers smile and shrug.

Then Bobby has a second thought. By paying a gondolier for a ride on the Venice canals, he would be supporting this jewel of a city so it can continue forever. He hands over the proper number of euros to one of the young gondoliers and climbs into the boat after Lisa.

As soon as they are settled, Bobby and Lisa lean into each other in the gliding gondola, taking in the full magic of Venice's twinkling lights against the darkening sky. The boat's easy rocking puts them in a contented trance. They turn to kiss as they pass Piazza San Marco.

Dear reader, it's me again, Nina. It's a joy to see my young Lisa in love!

This is what I say: We need to have more love—show more love—for this sad, angry world. It's the only thing that will save us. Love for our children, love for our neighbors, love for our parents and our grandparents. It's important for us to be close as families, as communities—don't you agree? What is happening to our world that I even need to say this?

For my heart, it's so good to see Lisa and Bobby together. But, reader, look—we are not alone. Watching them in their gondola is the winged lion. Do you see it up there in the shadows? It stands guard, protecting the piazza, majestic and proud among bright gold stars.

Ah, I see you are confused. With help from the writer here, let me explain. I tell you the winged lion is sleek, ferocious, powerful—it is the symbol for Saint Mark, who watches over Venice and its sailors, keeping them safe.

Saint Mark, also known as John Mark and Mark the Evangelist, wrote the second book of the New Testament, a quick story about the life of Jesus. Mark's mother had a house in Jerusalem, a frequent meeting place for early Christians, or so the story goes. Mark had a problem with Paul, but he made friends with Saint Peter, who shared many facts and stories, which Mark used in his writings.

Biblical experts—people who study it and know the history—doubt Mark himself actually heard Jesus speak. They say he described himself in Gethsemane when he wrote, "And there followed him a certain young man, having a linen cloth cast about his naked body; and the young men laid hold on him; and he left the linen cloth and fled from them naked."

So, you see, Mark is an important saint to Catholics like me. Most of us know his story. He lived in Alexandria, Egypt, for many years and may have been that city's church founder and first bishop. He died there as a martyr. Yes, it was awful—he was dragged through the streets by pagans.

Then, to add insult to injury, some of Mark's bones or relics were stolen from Alexandria by merchants and taken to Venice. They were eventually placed in a sarcophagus in the basilica bearing his name. Okay, not so bad.

You will see, dear reader, in paintings and sculptures, Mark is usually shown holding his book with a winged lion nearby.

Some say lions sleep with their eyes open. The lion image represents Jesus in Gethsemane, awake through the night before his crucifixion, and awake in his tomb. Did anybody keep Jesus company? No! What a shame on those disciples—they should have been right with him!

And so, dear reader, the bronze-winged lion looks down over Saint Mark's Square in Venice morning, noon, and night, keeping vigilant watch over the city and its many visitors. Tonight, it protects my dear Lisa and Bobby as they keep each other warm in that gliding gondola.

31

Colored Glass and Wild Cats

The next morning Lisa searches the wide waters, intent on identifying the number on an approaching vaporetto.

"That's it!" she cries to Bobby. They are waiting at a water bus stop on the Fondamenta Nuove for the boat that will take them to the other islands farther out in the lagoon within sight of Venice.

Their first stop—*If we manage to get on the right boat, thinks Bobby*, who is cranky because he missed his morning espresso—should be Murano. He did not know before this trip how energetic Lisa is about seeing sights. Sometimes he can barely keep up. Why did he let her start their day without him having coffee first?

Soon they are on the water. The boat cuts swiftly through the dark waters as Venice's low, unimposing skyline recedes. The morning sunlight brightly bounces off the water. Lisa and Bobby huddle close, curious to see Murano's famous glass factories. Once they arrive, they hurry to the first *fornaci*, or kilns, they see just ahead.

Lisa pulls Bobby to the front of a small crowd. A traditional glassblowing demonstration is about to begin and she wants to see it all.

A bald, middle-aged man with a blue apron takes a glowing blob of glass on the end of a long, thin metal pipe and places it into the wide opening of a kiln, then he twirls it carefully in the heat. He pulls out the metal pipe and rolls the molten glass along a metal table, shaping it. He returns the glass to the kiln for a few moments, then pulls it back out to roll it once more on the metal table.

Now he stops and blows into the end of the pipe with deep, even breaths, causing the glass at the other end to bulge out. After several more turns in the kiln, the man shows the crowd how the delicate bottle is streaked with yellow and blue. Finally, he adds an orange strip of molten glass as a handle, and he holds the finished glass pitcher aloft for the observers to see. Bobby, Lisa, and the others applaud loudly.

"Bravo!" someone shouts, and the craftsman takes a small bow.

Afterward, Bobby and Lisa stroll down the narrow street, looking in the windows. Colorful vases, shot glasses, bowls, and glass-bead necklaces pull Lisa's attention. Bobby stiffens as Lisa says, "I really would love to buy—"

"We can't bring a big glass thing back with us," he interrupts.

"Well, I can have it sent to us, can't I?"

Bobby sighs. There is no arguing. Clearly, Lisa has fallen in love with these Murano glass pieces and won't be happy until she owns one—at least one. He follows Lisa as she darts into the store. Inside they see an array of colorful pieces. Staring in wonder, Lisa picks up a large bowl with blue, green, and white swirls. Bobby notices the price tag.

"It's a bit expensive, isn't it?" he whispers.

"Don't worry," the shop owner kindly says, overhearing him. "This is something you will treasure forever. Now, this bowl it is authentic, as are all my pieces. But not everything around here is . . . made here." She lowers her voice. "Most tourists don't realize some of the lace and glass sold here have been produced elsewhere and sold as Italian—but they aren't." Lisa notices the shop owner has a pleasant smile and long gray hair braided and curled on top of her head. She's wearing big glasses with purple frames, giving her the look of an artist. She is obviously Italian, but she speaks English fluently. "*This* glass is made the same way as a thousand years ago," the shop owner says, nodding at the pieces in the display. "To own one of these pieces is to hold something ancient in your hands—even if it were made today. Because, you see, we honor our traditions here."

Bobby views the glass pieces with a new appreciation. "For some of these pieces, a very thin line of gold or silver has been added, giving it a unique color," the shop owner points out. "It is really . . . art. If you buy one, my dears, you will be glad you did for the rest of your life."

Lisa quickly pulls out her wallet and Bobby does not protest.

Later they catch another vaporetto to the island of Burano, which is famous for the lace made there. Bobby successfully convinces Lisa to move past the shop windows and follow him through the back streets, where brightly colored houses line the canals. Neither of them can resist buying a bag of cookies from a street vendor. "*Buranelli*," explains the seller, a grizzled old man wearing a wool vest and baggy pants. Later Lisa looks up the word and learns this biscuit is made only on Burano.

One more vaporetto ride takes them at last to the sleepy island of Torcello. Few people are about. *Is it lunchtime?* Bobby wonders.

"A kitty!" Lisa rushes toward a fat tabby, which darts away from her in a panic.

"There seem to be quite a few," Bobby says, pointing to about a dozen cats staring at them from a high wall nearby. "*Wild* kitties."

Lisa resists the temptation to pet one of the feral cats and instead gazes at them longingly from a safe distance.

After they stroll through the old Basilica di Santa Maria dell' Assunta, admiring its arched passageways and mosaics, they sit on a bench to eat their cookies.

"It's peaceful here," Bobby says, looking up at the pale blue sky dotted with white clouds. "It's as if time stopped." He stares at the pink brick walls and old trees with wide canopies that provide great pools of shade. Two seagulls squawk as they drift in a breeze overhead.

"Yes, but it *didn't* stop. We need to catch the boat back to Venice soon or we will be stranded here all night!" Lisa says. They crumple up their food bag and head back to the dock at the yellow and white vaporetto stop.

"I know our plan is to go on to Florence soon," Bobby says as they wait for their vaporetto, "but I could stay here in Venice . . . for a long, long time."

Lisa laughs in agreement. "Whew, I'm tired. I need to take a nap at the hotel."

"While you rest, I'm getting my espresso—the one I missed this morning," Bobby says.

"I'm sorry I rushed you," Lisa says. She makes a note to be

more mindful that her boyfriend—*No, wait, he's my husband!*—
needs his coffee in the morning.

RAVENNA

The honeymoon couple waits in the Ravenna train station,
feeling full and sleepy after eating bread and cheese they
purchased early that morning. Lisa and Bobby are heading to
Florence, but for now in the big, open train station they are
quiet as the slow minutes pass by.

Gray and white pigeons strut back and forth across the floor
in search of crumbs. Lost in their thoughts, Lisa thinks how
the pigeons are like tourists who travel back and forth across
Northern Italy in search of sublime food.

South of the Veneto region is the Emilia-Romagna region.
Its capital is Bologna, famous for the Quadrilatero, a lively area
of gourmet food shops.

The city of Parma is also in Emilia-Romagna. Parma features
the Teatro Regio, an old and revered theater where fine opera is
still performed. And Parma, of course, is the source of parmi-
giano cheese, eaten here with select cuts of ham.

And then there is Ravenna, a city with a dramatic history,
where Lisa and Bobby await their train. They have just spent
several happy days here.

"What was your favorite part of Ravenna?" Lisa asks. She
thinks about squacquerone cheese—like cream cheese with
tangy, luscious flavor. Bobby had to say the name again and

again with the help of a vendor before he got it right: "*skwah-ker-OWN-neh*." *I could eat it every day*, Lisa thinks. The first time she tried it at a little bistro, it was served with fresh ham on a *piadina*, a folded flatbread. Her mouth waters just thinking about this divine food in Ravenna.

"What did you say?" She hadn't been listening to Bobby's response.

"I said . . . the amazing Byzantine mosaics were my favorite part of Ravenna," Bobby repeats. "To think they made all those images with thousands of tiny pieces of stone and glass."

"And gold! I will not forget how the gold in the mosaics shimmered in the light."

"Didn't you love those mosaics of women saints lined up on one wall of Basilica di San Vitale, with the angels lined up on the other?" Bobby recalls the blue, green, and red mosaics in that sixth-century church. "Seeing art in Italy is different than in the US. Here it's very, very old, and most of it has religious meaning. It's not just art for art's sake."

He takes a swig from his bottle of mineral water and reflects on the mosaic imagery they saw in Ravenna. "Each mosaic symbolized some part of the life of Christ or a story from the Bible—it's like they were made to teach people or remind them about their lives as Christians."

"But they *are* works of art . . ." Lisa says.

"So is it art or a spiritual message?"

"Maybe both," Lisa says. "After all, doesn't beauty come from God?"

Bobby is surprised by this. He slowly nods, pondering how

Lisa's understanding of spiritual matters is far greater than his. *Hopefully, I will learn from her*, he thinks. His parents were artists who did not believe in religion, so spiritual symbols fascinate him because he knows little about them.

"And all those mosaics, made of thousands of tiny glass pieces, were created by human hands centuries ago, yet they are perfectly intact—at least most of them," Lisa says. "I guess that's why the city has eight UNESCO World Heritage sites."

"I'm glad we visited Ravenna," Bobby says. "Here it was always important to look *up*. The mosaics on the basilica ceilings are as elaborate as the ones on the walls and floors. Remember the dome inside the Neonian Baptistery with the mosaic of John the Baptist baptizing Christ?" The gold, green, and blue scene almost glowed, he says.

"It was just as important to look *down*," Lisa laughs. "Remember Domus of the Stone Carpets?" An entire Roman palace had long ago been discovered underneath Sant'Eufemia, a small church in Ravenna, as well as rooms and courtyards filled with mosaics—scenes of animals, dancers, and musicians frolicking in a way that hinted of a party-loving population.

"When I die, will you build a mausoleum for me like Galla Placidia's?" Lisa jokes, regally tossing her long hair over her shoulder. "Hers is incredible—that mosaic of little gold stars? The doves drinking water? All of it was so intricate, so beautiful."

"Well, she was a powerful woman of her time," Bobby laughs, "so of course I'll make sure your mausoleum is just like hers."

"Ravenna has everything: history, art, food, even beaches," Lisa declares.

"*Italy* has everything," Bobby says. He looks out over the train platform and recalls details of what he'd read about the city . . .

- Ravenna had been the capital of the western Roman Empire.
- In 540, the Byzantine general Belisarius ruled Ravenna, making the city a power center.
- There were revolts and invasions that led to Ravenna being controlled by the Lombards, the Franks, and . . . the pope!
- Ravenna joined Sardinia in 1859 and then became part of Italy in the reunification of 1861—maybe the most important date in Italian history.

Bobby smiles to himself. *Romans, Lombards, and Franks would laugh if they knew Ravenna would become an auto industry hub—what would they think of the sleek cars made by Ferrari, Lamborghini, Ducati, Maserati?*

A booming male voice over the loudspeaker suddenly announces the train to Florence is ready for boarding. The young couple jump up and head for the train.

Dear reader, it's Nina, butting in again. I am sorry, but I cannot be quiet!

I am watching my beloved granddaughter and her husband

get ready to board the train to Florence at high speed—too fast for me, I tell you! I like life to go more slowly.

Let me tell you a story.

When my children were growing up, they ran around our house and the farm all the time—fast! So, I made them come into the garden with me to pick berries. I told them to pick each one very carefully, so we could make jam. We needed each one! This made them slow down and pay attention. They liked the jam, and this taught them *a Dio piacendo*, how to slow down, how to be patient. Patience is very important, don't you agree? And when Lisa was a little girl, I taught her the same way. Slowly, slowly, pick each berry with care.

But now, allow me to tell you what I see from my heavenly view. Ravenna, this city Lisa and Bobby like so much, is in the Emilia-Romagna region, just inland from the Adriatic Sea—a canal connects the city to the sea. I had only a little education, but I did learn the ancient Romans liked Ravenna because it was a good port. They were smart! They made it a base for their navy. Don't let anyone ever say Italians aren't smart—we have intelligence in our genes.

La mia piccola Lisa, she is busy seeing all the special places . . . I hope she will visit the land of her ancestors, where my—our—family comes from.

FLORENCE

"*Firenze! Firenze!*" The train conductor's voice over the loudspeaker announces the approach of Florence, waking up Lisa and Bobby from their nap. They had fallen asleep almost as soon as they felt the soothing rock of the train car shooting along the tracks.

Now they quickly pull down their bags from the storage shelf. They plan to find a city bus to take them to their hotel—or rather, their room at a convent. Many convents and religious schools, they were happy to discover, now rent rooms out to tourists for far less money than a hotel.

After asking directions more than once, and walking around the same block twice, they purchase tickets at a newspaper kiosk, then wait for the bus. Finally, it pulls up and they get on, eager to see Florence from the high perch of their seats. It lumbers along the streets and boulevards until Bobby hears the driver call out the name of the intersection where they are to get off. At last they approach the convent, sign in with the Sister at the reception, and roll their suitcases down a long hall to their simple room. There, Bobby is happy to discover a shelf of books about Italy.

He picks out one about Italian painters and stretches out on the bed. "You know," he begins, "there is this idea of harmonic ratios in painting that Pythagoras first described—every painting was divided into sections that were related in a pleasing way."

He doesn't notice Lisa roll her eyes. Bobby has always loved Renaissance art—his college professor's enthusiasm was contagious, and Bobby's passion for it didn't end when that class was over. To Lisa's annoyance, Bobby insisted on bringing hard-cover art books that weigh a *ton* in their suitcase for this trip.

"And then Leon Battista Alberti took those principles to a whole new level. He compared design harmony with sound harmony . . . incredible," Bobby goes on.

"Bobby," Lisa stops him with an angry tone. He looks up at her in alarm. "I can't stand that you recite these facts to me all the time!" she says. "We're here in Italy *now*, not hundreds of years ago. Can't you be more in the present—with me?"

Bobby is stunned. He leaps up from the bed and goes to Lisa, who had been looking out the convent window at a small courtyard below. He wraps his arms around her shoulders. The air coming in from the window is cool and fresh. The *popolo di Firenze* walk quickly to their jobs and errands along the street near the courtyard.

"Okay, I will be in the present with you," he says good-humoredly. "I didn't know my reading bothers you. It's interesting to me, so I assumed it was interesting to you too."

"It is . . . just not *all the time*."

They have tickets to the Uffizi Gallery and they should get ready to leave, but they linger to stare at the courtyard and busy street.

"Can I tell you just one more thing about Alberti?" Bobby asks gently, and Lisa agrees with hesitation. "Leon Battista Alberti compared *sound harmony* with *design harmony*. The Renaissance was all about pleasing ratios and harmonies."

"Alberti . . . he was born here?" Lisa asks. She has to admit,

Bobby's enthusiasm sometimes inspires her to learn what made him so excited. Looking down at the stone building across the street, she half expects to see Alberti walk out of a doorway and wave hello.

"Alberti was born in Genoa in 1404," Bobby continues cautiously. He doesn't want to push his luck with Lisa by adding another story. "By all accounts, he was clever and daring. He wrote poetry and books about architecture, painting, and sculpture. And Alberti, when he was twenty, hoodwinked society by writing a Latin comedy and then claimed it was a rediscovered Roman antiquity. A lot of people believed him, apparently. Alberti traveled throughout Europe, and when he was twenty-four he found his way to Florence, where he made friends with the great thinkers of his generation—including Filippo Brunelleschi."

"Ha! I can almost see them—best Renaissance buddies," Lisa says.

"We will see it today at the Uffizi, I'm sure. Principles of perspective draw viewers into a painting, into a three-dimensional world with a vanishing point, where parallel lines converge on a distant horizon . . . Just remember, this all came from Italians," Bobby teases.

"What about . . . what's it called, chiaroscuro?" Lisa says, referencing the play of light and dark on a canvas that painters use for dramatic effect.

"Ah, yes," Bobby replies. "I don't think there is a word for it in English. And what a beautiful Italian word it is—*chiaroscuro*."

Lisa tries hard not to roll her eyes. Suddenly she's impatient to get moving again. "Okay, okay, let's get over to the Uffizi. We should have left an hour ago!"

Bobby is quite aware he's already spouted enough history for Lisa's tolerance, so he keeps his next thought to himself: *The Uffizi holds great art, yes, but it is a piece of art itself.* They walk at Lisa's fast pace through the streets, and he daydreams about its history.

The Uffizi was designed by the great Italian artist and architect Giorgio Vasari, who was born in 1511 in Arezzo. A well-known painter and historian, Vasari was hired to design and build palace administrative offices—*uffici*—for the state of Tuscany by Cosimo I de' Medici. The result is now known simply as the Uffizi.

Bobby and Lisa stand in line for a long time. He stares at the staircase filled with tourists waiting to get in. "It's one of the little-known circles of hell Dante wrote about," he jokes, "the interminable line to get into the Uffizi."

Lisa ignores him, craning her neck to see how close they are to the entrance.

Bobby recalls reading a book in college by Vasari called *The Lives of the Most Excellent Painters, Sculptors, and Architects*—biographies of Italian artists of the time, as well as descriptions of techniques they used—first published in 1550 and since translated into many languages.

Finally, they slowly progress up several staircases into the hallways of the famed museum. Bobby trails Lisa, lost in thoughts about the surrounding artworks, until suddenly he's aware Lisa has brought them in front of a huge painting.

"When I look at this painting, I am moved—emotionally and spiritually. What about you?" a woman's strong voice breaks into Bobby's thoughts.

They stand before the canvas entitled *Primavera*, also known as *The Allegory of Spring*, by Alessandro di Mariano di Vanni Filipepi Botticelli—better known as Sandro Botticelli, or just Botticelli.

The woman speaking is tall with dark hair and a striking red scarf around her neck. According to her name tag, her name is Sylvie—and she is not a guide but one of the museum's curators. She is leading a small group of elite visitors through the Uffizi.

"Let's follow her," Lisa whispers. Bobby nods in agreement and they quietly drift along the periphery of the group to eavesdrop. This way he and Lisa can discreetly head off on their own whenever they wish.

"This canvas is huge, as you can see—approximately six feet high and eight feet wide—so when you place yourself squarely before it, you almost feel like you can step right into the scene," the curator says, and a few men lean in to look more closely. A nearby guard takes notice and watches sternly.

"Youthful male and female characters with pale skin, red hair, and lithe bodies are gathered together lightly clothed, surrounded by a dark grove of orange trees. And you see here, Cupid hovers above," Sylvie continues. She points to one of the flowering plants at the bottom. "Botanists have identified five hundred plants in the painting. There is a lot to see just in this one allegorical painting, which is said to represent the triumph of love and reason over lower instincts."

Bobby and Lisa stare at the canvas, captivated.

"Botticelli was born in Florence in 1444, where he lived almost his whole life. He painted portraits, many commissioned by the Medici family, and Madonna paintings, using round canvases—profitable sources of income for many Renaissance painters. His Madonna figures are as beautiful as the women in his allegorical paintings—young with pale skin and delicate features.

"Even today, when I stand before the *Primavera*, I often lose track of the time," Sylvie says. "The scene is magical, inviting. The figures of the young men and women in their shimmery clothing and loose, wavy hair are joyful, beautiful, and sensuous. You get the sense that Cupid will undoubtedly work his magic to bring some of them together."

Lisa squeezes Bobby's arm and smiles up at him.

"We might thank Botticelli's muse for some of his greatest paintings," Sylvie continues. "Her name was Simonetta Cattaneo Vespucci."

What is a muse exactly? Lisa wonders. Fascinated by this idea, she drifts into a daydream. Lisa imagines how this muse might look and what she might say. What if the muse called Simonetta could be here, right now, to explain herself?

"Excuse me, ladies and gentlemen," the beautiful Simonetta

might begin, turning her pale face toward her small audience, her white robes flowing. "I am the muse for Sandro Botticelli. Without me, who knows if you would be standing here, admiring his paintings?"

Simonetta gently pulls a strand of red hair away from her oval-shaped face and smiles flirtatiously.

"A muse is a person—often a beautiful woman—who captivates and motivates the artistic sensibility, spurring an artist to create," Sylvie explains in Lisa's fantasy. "The concept comes from Greek mythology that claims nine daughters, or muses, were the offspring of Zeus and Mnemosyne, the goddess of memory. The muse named Thalia served to inspire comedy, Calliope inspired epic poetry, Terpsichore inspired dance and chorus singing, et cetera. Each muse had a specialty of inspiration.

"But a muse can be very much a warm-blooded human being," Simonetta interjects with a sly smile. "And Sandro Botticelli found his muse in me when I was a young woman. You can see me . . ." She blushes. "I am the redheaded subject of Botticelli's most famous painting, The Birth of Venus. *I modeled for many of his paintings. You see, I was a young noblewoman who came to Florence with her husband, where I became famous for my beauty. Botticelli fell in love with me." She glances at her listeners with a proud smile. "As did Giuliano Medici. Many men loved me . . . In 1475, the prize at a jousting tournament in the Florentine Piazza Santa Croce was a flag bearing my portrait painted by Botticelli. Just a year later, at twenty-two, I died of tuberculosis."*

The crowd sighs with disappointment.

"Botticelli wanted to be buried near me, and his wish was granted. We both rest in Florence at Chiesa di San Salvatore in Ognissanti. Such is the power of a muse."

Lisa shakes her head, her fantasy vanishing.

A group of Japanese tourists walks by. Sylvie says, "Come along, everyone! Fra' Filippo Lippi awaits us!"

When I was a young girl—fourteen, I think—I was in love with a boy in my village. Dear reader, his name was Gino. He and his brother, Lorenzo, both had red hair, like Botticelli's muse—it was unusual for anyone in Sicily.

Gino was my age, so kind and handsome, and even though I hardly spoke to him, I loved him from afar. He was slim, shyer than the other boys, and he had the sweetest smile. His parents were farmers too, but they lived several miles away. I only saw Gino at the market on Saturdays. Sometimes we talked about the animals in our village—he had a horse he loved, and I had two cats I adored.

Then for a few weeks he didn't appear, and I heard he was sick—a fever. An old woman in the village was giving him herbs for medicine, but they didn't work. And he died. I was devastated! My mother tried to comfort me, but I was so sad. One afternoon, I went to church and didn't tell anyone. The village church was very old, and always cool and dark inside. That day, the sunlight shined faintly through the three stained-glass windows.

The church was empty, so I found a painting that was propped up in a niche. I had seen it many times—it was a dark blue painting of the Mother Mary with the baby Jesus sitting on her lap. I kneeled in front of it and prayed for Gino. I prayed that Gino's spirit was happy, that he could see his horse from heaven, and that somehow he would let me know he was all right. I told God I would never forget Gino with the red hair and the shy smile—and I haven't.

That night when I went to bed, I had trouble falling asleep. I heard a commotion outside. My father and some other men were shouting—I got up and looked out my window. There was Gino's horse! It had broken free from its pen and came all the way to our side of the village. I ran outside, put my arms around the horse's neck, and stroked his head. Gino's father was there and gently pulled the horse away to take him home.

I tell you this because I believe it was the painting that took my prayers and sent them to heaven so Gino could hear them. And Gino was telling me he was all right.

Remember this, dear reader, when you go to Italy, to the museums in Florence and Rome, and see the beautiful paintings. Many people have prayed before them, and they have answered those prayers.

Oh, and you know, many years later, I married Gino's brother, Lorenzo. He was very sweet too. *Mio Amore*. He is here in heaven too, but he is quiet, not like me.

Lisa and Bobby, still following the little tour group, stop at *Madonna and Child with Two Angels*. "Where did Botticelli learn to paint? From Fra' Filippo Lippi, another Florentine," Sylvie explains to the group. "It inspires a spiritual awe, don't you think?"

Bobby thinks the young Mary looks to be a teenager. She tenderly gazes upon the baby Jesus, who has pudgy arms and legs. An impish angel looks out from the canvas right at viewers with a smile, as if inviting everyone to enjoy the intimate scene.

"The characters here, they seem about to speak," Sylvie notes. "There is a closeness between the mother, child, and the angels that brings you into a spiritual place of comfort, love, forgiveness."

Bobby looks at the painting for so long, he forgets he is in a museum at all. When he finally turns away, he doesn't know how long he's been standing there. He spins around, trying to get his bearings. He feels momentarily dizzy and takes a deep breath to collect himself, leaning against the wall to regain his balance. He reaches for Lisa's hand.

Sylvie announces it's time for a lunch break. Bobby and Lisa slip away to find the museum bistro already crowded, so they line up to get a table. They are finally seated when Lisa sees Sylvie standing in line. She waves to her and calls out, "You are welcome to share our table!"

Sylvie smiles and comes over to join them. "*Grazie*," she says. "I didn't realize it would be so crowded today." After ordering her lunch, she says, "I saw you were listening to my little talk. How do you like the paintings so far?"

"We love them," Bobby says. "Except . . . I nearly fainted. I had to hold on to the wall. I'm not sure what happened."

Sylvie laughs. "You were overwhelmed! Do you know the story of how the writer Stendhal fell over from seeing the great art in Florence in 1817? Yes, he fell! He wrote about it. As he stepped into the Basilica di Santa Croce with wonder—just as visitors do today—he looked up at the frescoes by Volterrano, which appear to ride on clouds out of the ceiling. Suddenly, he was so overwhelmed that he went into a state of ecstasy."

Bobby and Lisa laugh. They can relate.

"His heart beat fast and he stumbled. He later explained he had 'reached that point of emotion where the heavenly sensations of the fine arts meet passionate feeling.' You see, being so close to such a concentration of astoundingly beautiful art simply flooded his senses."

"Well, these paintings were not intended to be in one location," Bobby says. "They were meant to hang in individual churches all around the country, isn't that right?"

"Exactly," Sylvie says. "If you walked into a church and gazed at one or two paintings, you could take in their meaning and their emotional power, easily. But hundreds of paintings all in one hour or two? That is too much for a lot of people. And now this experience is called Stendhal syndrome."

Lisa's attention is riveted. It sounds like a psychology term, but she's never heard of it in any of her classes.

"An Italian psychiatrist in the Santa Maria Nuova hospital in Florence discovered in 1979 that more than a hundred patients over the previous decade had been brought to the hospital by ambulance directly from art museums and galleries, suffering palpitations and dizziness—symptoms similar to those experienced by the famous writer."

"Stendahl's reaction is understandable," Bobby says. "The sheer volume of art in galleries, museums, and churches in Italy is staggering. Look, we plan to see frescoes by Tiziano, sculptures by Michelangelo, portraits by Leonardo da Vinci, churches designed by Brunelleschi, paintings by Raphael, Caravaggio—all grand, beautiful, emotional."

"Ah, well, then . . ." Sylvie says with a smile, leaning forward. "I give you this word of caution. Give yourselves breaks in your art viewing. Go for an espresso or a dessert the moment you feel it's too much." Bobby and Lisa nod solemnly. "After all, Italy is meant to be enjoyed, not survived, don't you agree?"

At that moment, their food arrives at their table and the three begin to eat.

"You will enjoy the Caravaggio paintings we will see after lunch," Sylvie says, picking up her glass of Pellegrino. "He is a wonderful character. He was in his twenties when he painted a few of his masterpieces. And you know, Caravaggio had several encounters with death and suffering."

"Wasn't he from Milan?" Lisa asks. She admires Sylvie's style—her simple black dress and red scarf. The way she speaks and carries herself—Sylvie seems aristocratic.

"That's right," Sylvie says. "Born in 1571 in Milan. Then he traveled all over Italy, running from trouble or seeking work his entire short life. When he was eleven, Caravaggio was orphaned and he went to work as an apprentice to a painter in Milan. In 1592, he wounded a police officer during a fight and fled to Rome, arriving with little money and clothing."

"So, he was wild?" Bobby asks.

"Maybe, but was he really?" Lisa questions. "Could a reckless person be such a precise artist?"

"Ah, you see why I think he is so interesting. He was both," Sylvie says. "Caravaggio perfected the techniques of realistic painting. Then in a few years, he went on his own and made friends with artists of both high and low society. His paintings were offensive to some people, and sometimes they were rejected outright, but people loved them."

As Bobby and Lisa mull this over, Sylvie stands and says, "I must get back for the group. Please, join us if you can!"

"We will!" Lisa says, again noticing Sylvie's elegance as she walks away. *I hope I look that good when I get older.*

Dear reader, I know, I know, I keep interrupting, but I must say something.

Look at these young people, how smart they are! My Lisa, you won't find her scrubbing floors or milking cows. No, young women today, they want to see the world! Yes, this generation, they are really learning things here, seeing all this art—the best anywhere in Europe! I do not exaggerate when I say my country has the best art in the world. Do you want to argue with me? No, I didn't think so.

This place, the Uffizi, they should guard it more than a bank—they probably do, undercover, and we don't see it. Because the treasures here are worth more than money. It's not just the beauty, but look at these religious scenes with Mary and Gabriel, Mary and the baby Jesus, Jesus on the cross, Jesus being taken down from the cross—*che Dio ci perdoni!*

But the day is not over, and look, Lisa and her new husband are so healthy and strong. They still have energy to see more in this place.

I will be quiet . . . for now.

Caravaggio: The Popular Unpopular Painter

Sylvie has already moved on to the next gallery when Bobby and Lisa catch up.

"You will be absolutely mesmerized by this Caravaggio painting, *The Entombment of Christ*," she says. Her voice is quiet, as if she is sharing a secret or something holy. "Notice how the white body of Jesus, held by his friends Nicodemus and John, sprawls horizontally at an awkward, unnatural angle." Sylvie points to the huge, dramatic painting. "His flesh is drained of color and his right arm dangles limply above a stone slab that seems to jut out of the canvas, cold and hard." Now she steps to one side and angles her finger higher. "That is Mary standing to the right, with her arms raised and her eyes looking up. It's as if she is beseeching God for an explanation—'*Why did you let this happen?*'"

Bobby and Lisa are drawn in, feeling the gravity of this tragedy. Lisa winces, finding the brutal scene upsetting.

"It was commissioned as an altarpiece for the church of Santa Maria in Vallicella—also called Chiesa Nuova—in Rome, and painted by Michelangelo Merisi da Caravaggio, otherwise known simply as Caravaggio." She says solemnly, "The painting confronts us with Christ's humanity and his painful death by crucifixion, depicted in vivid realism. This is not an idealized depiction. The body of Jesus looks heavy, doesn't it? It's as if it could fall out of his friend's grip at any moment. Caravaggio was very different from other Renaissance painters in that his figures are natural, intensely real. Here, see how Nicodemus's fingers dig into the open wound on the dead man's torso? It's a cringe-worthy detail—that's how one American described it."

Lisa smiles at this last phrase.

"The reason why this painting is so arresting hundreds of years after it was completed—around 1603 to 1604—is precisely why Caravaggio was so controversial," Sylvie continues. "The faces, bodies, and scenes he painted were dramatic because they are *human*, not idealized. In *The Entombment of Christ*, you can feel the chill of Jesus's dead body, the terrible, unwieldy weight. How does Caravaggio do this? With dark, shadowy backgrounds and bright areas of light."

"Chiaroscuro," Lisa whispers to Bobby.

"Chiaroscuro," Bobby whispers back with a smile.

"Caravaggio puts viewers right in the middle of this disturbing encounter with death. It's almost as if he is saying, 'Look at this awful thing we've done!'"

Bobby nods, appreciating the painting more and more. He refocuses on it, seeing what the curator is talking about. He shivers.

"His masterpieces were admired for their dramatic composition and play of shadow and light; they were criticized for their shockingly realistic portrayals. Caravaggio painted men and women with wrinkled and worried faces, pale skin, protruding ribs, and scruffy, uneven beards. He painted effeminate young men and sexually suggestive Cupids. He painted laborers, card-players, and fortune tellers from lower social classes. He painted the decapitated heads of John the Baptist and Goliath in gory, bloody detail, the snake-covered head of Medusa with a face of horror."

Bobby thinks about the artist's adventures, how he lived outside and inside society and its laws. He wishes for a moment that he could talk to him, hang out with him and hear his stories.

"In May 1606, Caravaggio was wounded in a fight and killed a man," Sylvie says. "He fled to Napoli—Naples—where he continued his painting career."

"Did you hear that?" Bobby whispers to Lisa. "*NAH-polee.*

That's how to pronounce that city's name." Lisa nods as the curator continues.

"In 1608, Caravaggio was arrested and put in prison—but he escaped."

Of course he did, Bobby thinks. *He was smart, a survivor.*

"When he got out, he traveled to Sicily to meet an artist friend, but soon had to escape that region too. He returned to Naples and went on to paint several more masterpieces. The following year, in 1610, he died—many believe he was murdered."

"What a character!" Bobby says. "A dangerous criminal, a daring artist, a man on the run."

Later that night, Bobby falls asleep in the hotel room with a book about Caravaggio on his chest. As his breathing slows, he drifts into a dream.

"He was so rebellious and uncontrolled in his private life," the art historian Howard Hibbard tells Bobby as they sit next to a trickling stream somewhere in the Tuscan countryside. Howard is dressed uncomfortably in a suit. In the distance, Bobby glimpses a red-haired woman dancing behind a tree. She peeks out and waves to him.

The grassy bank is soft. Howard, an older gentleman with white hair, speaks loudly, as if delivering a lecture.

"Wait, are you talking about Caravaggio?" Bobby interrupts.

"Yes, who do you think I mean? Of course, Caravaggio! I've written a book about him, haven't I? Didn't you finish it yet? It was part of your assignment."

"The assignment? Uh, no, but I will," Bobby says, feeling guilty.

"As I was saying . . . Caravaggio was sensual, daring, free, wild, yet he produced technically proficient and dramatic paintings. I don't think you even know the extent of his work. He was a true artist—in so many ways!" Howard bursts out. "He had to paint."

Now he stands and begins pacing up and down along the stream, shouting at Bobby. "Unpredictable though he was, Caravaggio was serious, almost businesslike about his commissions!"

"You act like I'm disagreeing with you, but I'm not. I'm very interested," Bobby says.

"All right, but I want to make sure you understand why every generation is attracted to his art. He worked very hard, produced his work close to the time specified, regularly met his contractual obligations with only minimal delay. Don't forget, this was quite different from the procrastination of many artists. And as I wrote in my book—if you ever finish it, you will see—Caravaggio's innovative style, even at its most classic, was difficult for the public to assimilate and was even considered deliberately rude, confrontational. His disregard for traditional decorum led some to reject his works."

Bobby stands up on the grassy stream bank. "I must go, Mr. Hibbard. I am waiting to find out if I got a job back at home. I'm very nervous about it and I am supposed to find out soon if I get it—"

"A job?" Howard says. "Oh, I heard you are one of the top candidates for it."

"How do *you* know?" Bobby is incredulous.

"I have my connections," Howard says, nodding his head seriously. "Well, be on your way, then!"

Remembering his manners, Bobby says, "Thank you for talking to me about Caravaggio. I do need to get back to the Uffizi—I think Lisa and I must visit Caravaggio's *The Entombment of Christ* again."

Howard looks up at the blue sky, then smiles. "I apologize if I've gone on and on. It's always good to know about the artists' lives, the way they thought, the way they lived. Please say hello to your lovely wife for me—and good luck with the job!"

"Thank you," Bobby replies with bewilderment, watching Howard stroll away.

Bigger than Life: Michelangelo's David

Bobby tries to tell Lisa about his dream the next morning, but she is determined to see Michelangelo's *David*.

There is just too much art and too little time to see it all! Bobby thinks with a groan.

He and Lisa are soon walking briskly along Via dei Calzaiuoli, looking into the elegant shop windows. Florence— *Firenze*—what a beautiful place to be first thing in the morning! The sunlight warms the air as it brightens the walls of the stone buildings.

Suddenly, the Duomo looms ahead. They slow their pace to stare at the massive green and white marble structures of the Cattedrale di Santa Maria del Fiore and the famous red dome ingeniously designed and engineered by Filippo Brunelleschi. Bobby and Lisa twirl like children, taking in the size and beauty of the entire plaza. It promises to be a beautiful day, and they are eager to start their adventures. But first—

"I need an espresso," Bobby says, leading them across the piazza to find a small round outdoor table at a bistro. "*Per favore*, can you tell us—what is that building?" he asks the waitress when she comes to their table. He gestures to the octagonal building.

"*Battistero di San Giovanni!*" she replies with a laugh, as if everyone knows this. "It is . . ." She struggles to find the English words. "It is a place of *battesimo*—baptism. Saint John—as you say, John the Baptist—is the patron saint of Firenze." Then she adds proudly, "It is *uno dei più antichi* . . . one of the oldest buildings in Firenze."

"Amazing," Lisa says appreciatively. "John the Baptist . . . He's the one who had wild hair, ate locusts, and announced the arrival of Jesus. I bet if he were to appear in this piazza right now in front of the building named for him, he would be arrested!"

"And yet he looks over Florence. He was chosen to be the city's saint."

"*Per favore*," Lisa starts, ready with another question once the waitress returns with their coffee on a tray with a bowl of sugar cubes and tiny spoons. "*Quando è la festa di San Giovanni?*"

The young waitress replies with a smile, "*Ventiquattro giugno.*"

Lisa thanks her, then turns to Bobby. "June twenty-fourth. I hear they shoot off fireworks from the Ponte Vecchio and have events the whole day. Too bad we will be in Rome by then."

Bobby sips his espresso and stares at the passersby. "I know we said this about Venice, but I could live here in Florence for a year, or more—couldn't you? It's deeply satisfying to see the art and the buildings in person, after having read about them."

Lisa nods emphatically. "But let's go—I want to see Michelangelo's *David*."

"I'm ready!" Bobby says. After carefully counting out the correct number of euro coins to leave on the table, they hustle off toward the Accademia Gallery.

Finally, they see it: *David* is a seventeen-foot-tall, twelve-thousand-pound white marble statue carved by Michelangelo Buonarroti. It portrays a naked yet fearless young man with a slingshot in his right hand, ready to take on the giant Goliath. Michelangelo completed the masterpiece in 1504.

Lisa and Bobby stop, stunned at the size of the sculpture they'd seen in so many photos. Though it is oversized, the statue is eerily realistic—the vein on the back of David's left hand almost seems to pulsate. Every muscle in the youthful figure appears taut, yet his stance is relaxed and confident. Michelangelo finished the sculpture when he was twenty-nine years old, and some believe it represents the sculptor at the height of his artistic career: youthful and already larger than life.

Lisa spots a young tour guide leading a group of elderly British tourists. "I know you don't like tours, but let's just listen for a moment," she whispers to Bobby.

"When viewing *David*, you see the sculptor's extraordinary skill in carving this confronting, larger-than-life figure out of rough stone," says the guide, who wears a tweed jacket and carries a silly little stick with a yellow flag on top so his group can follow him. "In Michelangelo's lifetime, Florence was the center of art. His talent was recognized by Lorenzo de' Medici—a man who appreciated poets, artists, and intellectuals, and he took the sculptor under his wing. But Michelangelo traveled to other cities—Bologna, Rome—and he began *David* in 1501, when he was just twenty-six. He was famous by then, the highest-paid artist of his time."

As she gazes, awestruck, at the commanding statue, Lisa remembers the story from Sunday school. David had only a slingshot and five smooth stones taken from a brook when he was challenged by Goliath, who was dressed in full armor and carried a spear. But with that simple slingshot, David launched a stone that hit Goliath square on the forehead. Goliath dropped to the ground, dead. David cut off the head of the dead Goliath and brought it to Jerusalem in victory.

"Before this work, other artists had only depicted David *after* he slayed Goliath," the guide continues. "Never had the Biblical character been depicted *before* the fight. Michelangelo's *David* offers inspiration. This is a bold and daring confrontation with an enemy, and an ambitious will to fight Goliath, a powerful adversary."

"He looks courageous," Bobby says with admiration. "Calm and ready."

"I think it's embarrassing," Lisa whispers loudly to Bobby. "He—*it*—is completely naked!"

The guide hears Lisa and glares at her, then continues: "The nakedness of this statue makes some viewers uncomfortable. It is said that when the Grand Duke of Tuscany presented Queen Victoria a cast of the statue in 1857, the queen immediately donated it to a museum and commissioned a fig leaf to be made to cover David's genitalia."

Dear reader, I know, I know—I said I would be quiet. But I must say something. Do we need to see this statue completely naked—is this necessary? I don't think so. What about the children? What does the pope think? I'm sure the nuns would not approve.

I am watching Lisa and Bobby circle around this David—goodness, they are very curious about Italian art. I don't blame them—these are the works of masters.

And all these visitors . . . I tell you, we Italians are quite used to tourists. In fact, they put food on our tables when they come to eat in our restaurants, sleep in our hotels, fill our museums.

Even before I was born, people were coming to Italy for its beauty, its art. And there was a time when rich people in particular made it essential for their children to tour our galleries.

Here, I will let the writer explain:

Young men from aristocratic families in Britain traveled a

particular European route called the Grand Tour. It was part of a rich person's education a long time ago in the seventeenth and eighteenth centuries. The trips were designed to introduce the young men to a wealth of art and antiquities in countries different than their own.

The senses, stimulated by the outer world, caused people to reflect and form ideas, which ultimately led to understanding, according to the British philosopher John Locke. Therefore, exposure to great art could lead to knowledge.

After touring Belgium, Switzerland, and France, where these wealthy young men got lessons in riding and fencing, they traveled to Italy, along with their chaperones and servants. They visited Pisa, Milan, and Rome—with a sensuous side trip to Venice—but they spent several months in Florence, visiting museums, galleries, and the salons, seeing paintings and sculptures. Renaissance art was what they really wanted to see.

Other visitors see art as something religious, spiritual. Christian themes—well, these have special, deep meaning for all followers of this religion. The scenes in the paintings represent critical moments of Christianity.

Paintings that once hung in church niches around the country are today clustered in museums, where they can be viewed together in a matter of days—maybe that's precisely why some people faint, as Bobby almost did in the Uffizi. It's like having all the churches in one place; the concentration of art is almost too much to take in. But this was not how it was intended to be viewed.

Mud Angels

A dramatic event that all Italians of a certain age remember well happened on November 4, 1966. Heavy rainwaters overflowed into the streets of Florence, destroying fourteen thousand works of art and damaging even more. The heroic effort of young Italian people to save their country's art is a story Italians are eager to tell, and indeed everyone should know it because it is one of courage and hope.

After weeks of heavy autumn rainfall, levees broke, surging the waters of the Arno River throughout the city. Muddy water mixed with fuel oil flooded the National Library, churches, museums, and the city's entire historic center.

Streets became rivers of rushing water, sweeping cars into the Piazza Santa Croce, where they bumped into each other, turned upside down, and piled up in metallic heaps. Citizens scrambled to safety as the water level rose swiftly.

Caught by surprise and with no emergency flood plan in place, government officials were slow to respond. But young people leaped into action. They flocked to Florence from around Italy and even other countries to retrieve paintings, artifacts, and rare books from the mud. They created human chains, pulling treasures out of the mud in the National Library and passing them hand-to-hand to dry land. One journalist who witnessed this spontaneous act of aid called the young people "Mud Angels," and the name stuck.

Filmmaker Franco Zeffirelli made a documentary about the

rescue effort, *Florence: Days of Destruction*, with Richard Burton narrating in English and Italian. "I'm Richard Burton," he began his Italian version. "You will forgive my imperfect Italian, but I would like to try to speak to you without translation because what happened in Italy and in Florence concerns me deeply."

When the film was shown around the world, $20 million in donations poured in for the restoration of Florence's damaged artwork and archives. Today, visitors in Florence will notice plaques high up on the walls of public and private buildings, indicating how high the flood waters rose and the magnitude of the catastrophe.

And when damage like this happens, the other heroes are conservationists, without whom much of the world's great art might be lost forever.

One painting badly damaged in the 1966 flood was of the Virgin Mary with the infant Jesus: *The Madonna Presents the Christ Child to Santa Maria Maddalena de' Pazzi*. It was painted by the female portrait painter Violante Beatrice Siriès Cerroti, who lived from 1710 to 1783. The painting looked fine from the front. But a creeping mold was growing right underneath the paint. The damage went unnoticed for decades while the painting hung in a niche of the sacristy altar in the church of Santa Maria Maddalena de' Pazzi in Florence.

It was rescued from complete ruin just in time. In 2016, Elizabeth Wicks and Nicoletta Fontani, two Florentine art conservators, took the painting down from the niche and quickly discovered the extensive mold damage. The two women began the slow, painstaking process of restoration, which Wicks recounted in the book *La Signora Pittrice: The Lady Who Paints—Violante Siriès Cerroti*, published by Pacini Editore.

It's almost impossible to imagine the delicate and patient work required of conservationists. Wicks and Fontani removed the grime and mold, repaired holes and edges of the canvas, and re-stretched the painting on a new frame so it could be properly displayed and seen in all its restored glory.

The Cerroti painting is actually a copy of one painted by Luca Giordano. Artists who were skilled at copying others' work were highly regarded during the Renaissance, contrary to modern sentiment about copying as an inferior art. "Before the advent of photography and other methods of reproduction, artists were often commissioned to paint copies, whether of their own or other's works," writes Wicks, who is American born but now a longtime resident of Florence. "Painting manuals, from that of Cennino Cennini onward, cite copying as the foremost method of learning to draw and paint. All artists, male and female, trained by copying other artists' works. For early women artists denied the privilege of drawing nude models or copying classical sculpture collections, in venues such as the Uffizi Gallery, copying portraits or religious paintings was an especially valuable learning method. Historically, a good copy could be appreciated in its own right, sometimes even achieving a status on par with the original."

Italians are proud of their copying artists. When the German artist Albrecht Dürer learned someone was copying his series of woodcuts called *Life of the Virgin* in 1506, his search for that person took him to Italy, where he found Marcantonio Raimondi, an accomplished engraver in Venice.

Dürer sued Raimondi. The Venice court considered the fact that Raimondi's copies were not exact reproductions, but close; he included Dürer's "AD" signature, as well as his own.

The verdict? The Venetian court said Dürer should be flattered by the reproduction because it indicated his work was worth copying.

Bobby and Lisa walk along the wide, peaceful Arno River on their last afternoon in Florence. They are tired, their senses overwhelmed.

The Ponte Vecchio teems with pedestrians. It's late in the day and the sky is suffused with gold light as the sun begins to set. Florentines crowd the walkway on the river's edge, heading home or to a bar after work. This bridge was built in 1345, and it looks much the same today as it did centuries ago.

"I love piazzas," Lisa says. "They almost all have a fountain and lots of bistros." She and Bobby arrive at a bistro in Piazza Santa Felicita, grab a table, and sigh in relief as they sit. It's been a busy day. They order two bottles of Pellegrino.

"And piazzas are the ideal people-watching spots," Lisa continues, studying two women in tight skirts walking by, one with red heels, the other in lace-up boots. Then her eyes follow a woman holding a cotton grocery bag packed full of produce in one hand, her little boy's hand in the other. "Why don't American cities have public squares like this?" Bobby notices two old men walking small dogs, as they talk with great animation and hopelessly attempt to keep the leashes from tangling.

"It seems that in cities and little towns, piazzas are situated so everybody has to cross paths with everybody else at some point in the day," Lisa says, half talking to herself. She quietly watches the scene for a few minutes. "All these small neighborhoods are just so lively and fun—do you think they intentionally foster a sense of community? It makes everyone feel as if they belong. I'm thinking about resilience. If you feel like you belong somewhere, that your neighbors know you and your family and will watch out for you, wouldn't that make you feel like you could handle any kind of challenge in life?"

"Yes, I do," Bobby agrees as he watches the men with their dogs finally reach the other side of the piazza. They sit down on a bench, conversing all the while. "The streets are so narrow that they force people to acknowledge each other."

"Speaking of resilience, remember, I have to pick a thesis topic. My professor says it has to be really specific . . . I don't know what I'm going to do!"

"It will come to you. I have faith in you, Lisa," Bobby says. And he does. He is in awe of Lisa's intellect and ability to comprehend complex ideas. He loves this about her.

Later, he looks up more about the role of the piazza in one of his books. Images of piazzas, it turns out, have appeared in paintings for centuries.

"In or near the center of every town is the piazza," he reads in the Frederick Hartt book *History of Italian Renaissance Art*, "the great square which is the focus of civic life. It is, above all, essential to understanding the civic nature of Italian art. Surrounded by a natural world which man is constantly trying to dominate, Italian art is based on communication between people in the square and adjoining streets where the life of the community takes place. In those smaller Italian towns where the great squares have not become parking lots, this is still true."

Piazzas create the feeling of a small village, Bobby thinks. *You see everyone and everyone sees you.*

Forgotten No More: Artemisia Gentileschi

A flock of pigeons bursts up into the air, circles around, and lands on the cobblestones near a little girl and her mother tossing crumbs on the other side of the piazza.

"Ciao, *uccellini!*" the little girl shouts as the pigeons eagerly peck at the bread around her. Lisa gazes at the girl and her mother as if caught in a trance. Will she and Bobby have children one day? She hopes so.

Children seem easily integrated into daily life in Italy. They come with their families to restaurants and churches. They play in the street and help out in their parents' shops. They are looked after and loved, it seems, by family and neighbors.

Lisa's gaze turns to a young woman striding through the piazza. The woman wears a bright-colored dress and hat. Lisa smiles at her daring style—and suddenly she remembers a daring woman artist.

"There's something—someone—I want you to see," she

says, turning to Bobby with a mysterious grin. He gives her a quizzical look. "Follow me—I think you will like her."

She leads him by the hand along the Arno River. From the first conversation they had on their college campus five years ago, Lisa has known Bobby is open to adventure.

They approach the Pitti Palace on the south side of the river.

"Oh, I can't . . . another museum?" Bobby groans.

"I really want to see this one painting—just one." Lisa guides him through the entrance, then whisks him through the grand halls, finally stopping in front of *Madonna con Bambino*, a painting by Artemisia Gentileschi.

"Interesting," Bobby says, staring at the painting. "She does not look like other Marys we've seen. She's just a practical, down-to-Earth-looking woman focused on getting her baby to breastfeed."

"Yes, she's amazing—like a female Caravaggio," Lisa says. "I've read about her life. It is a made-for-TV movie if there ever was one!" She lowers her voice in the hushed museum. "She paints women in this very realistic way, sometimes in violent scenes. She was born in Rome in 1593—her father was a painter who taught her the trade, and they both studied Caravaggio's realistic style. Artemisia's teacher, Agostino Tassi, raped her. Later she moved to Florence, where she became very successful and made friends with Cosimo de' Medici—the Pitti Palace, where we now stand, was his house—and Galileo, the astronomer."

"Whoa, her life *does* sound like a movie—very dramatic." Bobby leans forward to get a closer look at *Madonna con*

Bambino. Nearby, a museum guard in a stiff uniform loudly clears his throat, as if to say, *You're getting a bit too close!*

"I like this painting a lot—I'd like to see more," Bobby says. "It's a Biblical scene, but it's as if she wants us to see Mary was a real person, not an ideal."

"This is the only painting of hers here," Lisa says. "I read about Artemisia and really wanted to see this. She's just been rediscovered by art lovers."

"I don't mean to change subjects," Bobby says after a moment, "but Florence is famous for its food—and I'm getting hungry."

"Me too, let's find a good place to eat!"

Preserving Italy

My dear reader, yes, it's Nina again. Are you enjoying this Italian adventure? It fills me with so many happy memoires.

For instance, my little garden in Sicily—how I loved it! When I married and had children, my garden gave me peace, even though it was small and took some work. Then, a long time after that, when I moved in with my daughter and her husband in America—Lisa's parents—they said I could plant a little garden there too. I loved that—a garden is a little piece of heaven—and I taught little Lisa how to plant seeds and take care of growing plants.

I think we Italians . . . we care for our gardens, our homes, the same way we care for our old aunts and uncles and grandparents. We treasure them, we respect them, we love them. In my lifetime, I saw this.

You don't believe me? Well . . . in Italy, preservation was written into Article 9 of our country's 1947 constitution: "The Republic promotes the development of culture and of scientific and technical research. It safeguards natural landscape and the historical and artistic heritage of the Nation." I know what I am talking about.

And in recent years, support for Italy's cultural preservation has come from fashion companies—*sì*, fashion!

You know, of course, the Colosseum. Well, I will tell you that construction began in 70 AD and it was made to seat fifty thousand people. Today, the Colosseum attracts more than four million tourists each year. So, you think it could be falling down by now, right?

But no! We should thank the fashion company Tod's, which makes fine leather shoes and goods. In 2011, Tod's paid more than $20 million for a big multiyear restoration, including the removal of layers of black soot.

They're not the only ones to step up for Rome's monuments. You know the Roman jeweler Bulgari? Very famous, yes? The company paid $1.7 million to clean and restore the travertine stones of the Spanish Steps. Fendi too spent more than $2 million to help restore Rome's famous Trevi Fountain.

You know, I, Nina, am long gone, but I watch what's happening from heaven above. I see what is happening with the land, the water. And I think, *Dio mio!* Save this country, this world! Plastic in the ocean? *Per favore, no!*

In Italy, I think, businesses and people are trying to preserve the land while still supporting the local economy. Stelvio National Park, in the central Alps, keeps up earth-friendly practices—and Val di Pejo, the ski area in the northern part of the park, has banned all plastic: bottles, plastic forks and knives, packaging, even ketchup packets. This was after researchers in the State University of Milan showed something terrible, that the nearby Forni glacier contains millions of plastic particles!

What are we doing? This plastic, do we need it so much? My mother and grandmother never had plastic in their kitchens, and now everybody thinks it is *molto importante*!

You know, I have heard that five hundred thousand tons of plastic—bottles, straws, bags—litter the Mediterranean every year. At least that's what the Italian Institute for Environmental and Protection Research says. I believe them.

So, the European Union voted to ban single-use plastic items in 2021. And now bars and restaurants give you alternatives to plastic straws made of paper, metal, or even uncooked tube-shaped pasta.

I agree with no plastic—but pasta straws? *Non per me, grazie!*

If Buildings Could Talk

"Every building has a story," Bobby muses. He is driving their rental car south, trying to keep his eyes on the winding road instead of the rolling countryside. He knows speeding upsets Lisa, but if she were not with him, he would be driving their Alfa Romeo *a lot* faster.

"If Italian buildings could talk, imagine the stories they could tell of all they have seen—especially here," he says.

"Very true," Lisa agrees. She's glad Bobby is up for the challenge of driving—and that he's staying within the speed limit. "Oh, here's one list of favorite buildings," she says, staring at an article on her iPad.

"Who made that list?" Bobby asks skeptically.

"Sylvia Hogg and Stephen Brewer—they're writers for *Frommer's Italy* guidebooks, so they should know."

"Okay, name their buildings."

Lisa begins: "There is the Pantheon. It sits right in the middle of Rome—"

"*ROE-ma*," Bobby corrects.

"*ROE-ma*, okay. The Pantheon was built in 27 BC, then rebuilt by the Roman emperor Hadrian in the second century AD. The huge dome is made of bricks and, incredibly, has an opening at the top through which rain, sunshine, and moonlight fall."

"I do know about the Pantheon," Bobby says with a bit of condescension.

"Then there is Villa D'Este, outside Tivoli—do you know of it? It was built in the middle of the sixteenth century by Cardinal Ippolito d'Este of Ferrara. The villa is ornate, but the big attractions are the vast gardens and elaborate fountains."

"What about Brunelleschi's Duomo in Florence?" Bobby asks.

"Yes, that's on the list—and we saw it!" Lisa says. "It was built between 1420 and 1436—a major engineering achievement."

"Is the Leaning Tower of Pisa on the list?" Bobby asks. "I read that it started leaning pretty soon after it was constructed about nine centuries ago—then probably the tallest bell tower in Europe. It has been reinforced many times since, thank goodness, so it's safe to climb."

"No, thank you," Lisa says. "The tilt would give me vertigo. But one place I'm happy to visit is Certosa di Pavia. That's a huge monastery in Lombardy with a Renaissance façade and interior frescoes, cells for the monks, and the mausoleum of Gian Galeazzo Visconti—the first duke of Milan. It's supposed to be spectacular."

"What about the lakes in the north, and islands?" Bobby

asks. "I want to see Palazzo Borromeo on Bella Island on Lago Maggiore—*LA-go Maj-OR-eh*—I've read it has amazing grottos below and terraced gardens above that overlook the water."

"I want to see Lake Como—*LA-go CO-mo*—where George and Amal Clooney live," Lisa adds. "Then there is Palazzo Te, the palace near Mantua designed by Guilio Pippi—who was also a painter, by the way, who studied with Raphael. That palace is full of art and artifacts. The wild Federico II Gonzaga, Duke of Mantua, lived there and commissioned erotic frescoes."

Bobby glances at her in surprise. "Erotic frescoes?"

"Yes! Then there is Palazzina di Caccia di Stupinigi, near Turin—a massive palace with 137 rooms and seventeen galleries, where the Savoy family stayed during their hunting adventures—a rather extravagant hunting lodge. There is a bronze stag standing above the domed pavilion. I'd love to see that."

"If Palazzina di Caccia di Stupinigi could talk, its story would be epic," Bobby sighs.

Hearing

MUSIC TO THE EARS

SIENA

"*Siamo in Toscana?*" Bobby practices Italian phrases as he drives. "*Toe-SCANN-ah*," he says, elongating the N. "I really want to say 'Tuscany' like an Italian," he says. "I learn more from hearing people speak Italian than I ever did from lessons."

"There is a lot to be learned by listening," Lisa says, watching the soft green hills as they pass. "Hearing is an underappreciated sense. If we could just be quiet for a few minutes, we could really hear the sounds of nature and life."

It is late afternoon when Bobby and Lisa spot Siena's famous rose-colored brick buildings in the distance, looking especially pretty in the golden sunlight. They drive up and down the narrow streets until they find their hotel, and after checking in, they head out to walk on the cobblestones, taking in the old city. Siena is not big—its population of year-round residents is less than sixty thousand—but its quaint beauty begs to be explored.

Bobby stops in front of a sign taped to a lamppost that describes Palio delle Contrade, a local bareback horse-racing event. The races last only a few minutes, but the celebrations last for days. Lisa imagines the sound of the horses galloping and the crowds cheering. Sounds, she has decided, are an entryway into every place they visit.

"Oh, too bad we missed it," Lisa says, noticing the date on the sign. "If only we'd known."

"I bet it is fun to watch," Bobby says, sharing her disappointment. He likes fast travel of any kind: by car, train, horse, and scooter.

Turning away, Lisa brightens. "Oh, look, an opera house!" She points to a solid stone building with steps symmetrically leading up to the entrance from either side. The late-afternoon light bathes it in pink and gold. She steps toward it and accidently bumps into an old man in a too-big jacket walking by with a cane, his arm linked with a younger woman who looks very much like him—his daughter, Lisa guesses. After apologizing profusely in what little Italian she knows, Lisa tries to explain that she was admiring the opera house.

"Ah, *sì, sì*," the old man says, nodding in a way that indicates, *Of course, an opera house is always worthy of admiration.* Lisa can't help but gush. "Italians are opera singers, composers, musicians, famous . . . *in tutto il mondo*."

Pleased by Lisa's enthusiasm, the old man smiles at them both, tips his hat, and continues walking with his daughter.

"Think of all the musical words that are Italian," Lisa continues as she and Bobby head over to the opera house. "*Tempo*, for time . . . *forte*, for loud . . . *piano*, for soft . . ."

"*Soprano, concerto* . . ." Bobby adds, getting into the spirit.

"And *bravo, brava*."

"It's true—everyone knows these terms," Bobby says. "If I remember correctly from my high school music course, we can thank an Italian Benedictine monk from the tenth century— Guido d'Arezzo—who came up with these terms."

"Guido d'Arezzo? Who was he?"

"He devised a musical notation system to help singers who had trouble memorizing hymns or chants. And . . . this system has been used by singers and musicians ever since."

After admiring the opera house from every angle, Lisa steers Bobby toward Piazza del Campo, the heart of Siena, from which spans a semicircle of stunning structures and monuments. The grandest one of all is the elegant Torre del Mangia.

"That means 'Tower of the Eater,'" Bobby translates.

"I overheard our hotel receptionist say it was named after its bell ringer—he was either very overweight or he spent too much money," Lisa says. Together, they laugh.

"And that reminds me—what is our dinner plan?" Bobby asks.

They gravitate toward a small restaurant nearby, its entrance covered with bright red bougainvillea. A waiter wearing a long white apron smiles and, without a word, leads them to a table.

Still intrigued by the story of Guido d'Arezzo, Bobby searches for more details on his phone. "Why isn't Guido d'Arezzo famous all over the world? All European music is based on his music notation system. Not only did he create that, but he also made a simple song to help singers remember notes. Wait . . . didn't Rogers and Hammerstein borrow from that song in *The Sound of Music*?"

"Doe, a deer, a female deer . . ." Lisa sings softly.

Bobby keeps reading as the waiter brings the bottle of wine Lisa ordered. "Guido d'Arezzo's musical notation system is music's universal language." He puts his phone down and sips the wine. "Another Italian who changed the world."

Across the street Lisa sees a well-dressed woman with dyed red hair standing in the doorway of her clothing shop. The woman hums loudly, nodding to passersby.

Whatever song is in her head, Lisa reflects, it is distantly related to Guido d'Arezzo.

The Joy of Singing

Did I tell you about my papà? Yes, it's Nina, interrupting again.

Just like his brother, my papà, Luigi, sang when he worked. This would be Lisa's great grandfather. He sang at home too, little folk songs, parts of operas he knew. I grew up hearing it, and it was like the birds chirping, just part of my life. I never had a voice for singing, but that didn't stop me. I would hum and sing just like my papà. Singing is just a way to feel better, to fill the heart with happiness.

Here, the writer wants to tell you something about music in Italy . . .

Italians often respond to emotional situations by singing. Music is embedded in the country's history, cultures, and everyday life. For example, *Festival di Sanremo*, a music competition, is the most-viewed TV show of the year. For an entire week, professional and amateur singers perform original songs, written for this one event. When the festival began in 1951, it was immediately popular. Today, it features a song contest, star singers, famous presenters, and completely unknown performers, all of whom walk a red carpet and celebrate their moment of fame. The show lives out a truth that Italians stand by, that singing unifies people and lifts the spirits of the singers and all who hear the songs.

When COVID first ravaged lives in Northern Italy in the spring of 2020, the blind Italian opera singer Andrea Bocelli performed in the empty Duomo in Milan for Easter. In the midst of the unfolding tragedy, Bocelli sang in that sacred space without an audience—except for the twenty million people who streamed the performance through their computers and phones. The setting of Milan, where thousands died from the coronavirus, made Bocelli's concert all the more poignant.

"On the day in which we celebrate the trust in a life that triumphs, I'm honored and happy to answer *sì* to the invitation of the city and the Duomo of Milan," Bocelli said in a brief introduction. "Thanks to music, streamed live, bringing together millions of clasped hands everywhere in the world, we will hug this wounded Earth's pulsing heart."

Bocelli was born in Lajatico, Tuscany, in 1958. He appeared in the Sanremo Festival in 1994, winning awards in the newcomer category. He went on to record many albums, and after recording a duet called "The Prayer" with Celine Dion, his name became known around the world.

Opera dramatizes every nuance of human experience, elevating them all to high art—an art that is emotionally captivating. Jealousy, betrayal, romance, tragedy, death—when these deep, stirring emotions are sung by powerful voices, they pull on listeners' hearts. "Italian opera is the ultimate expression of the collective Italian genius," Florentine composer Mario Ruffini once said. "The Italian sun captured in sound. It stems from the Italian nature, the Italian voice, the Italian soul."

"When did you start liking opera?" Lisa asks Bobby as they walk through Siena after dinner. She notices his dark hair has gotten longer on this trip; she likes the look.

"A friend of mine loved it, so I learned to understand it and like it very much," Bobby says.

"A friend?" Lisa asks, smiling. "What was her name?"

"Oh, uh, her name was Isabella."

"Why haven't you ever mentioned her before? Where did you know her?"

"She joined my class during my senior year in high school— her family had moved from Italy, but I don't know from where.

One time, she had friends over to her family's house and she played a CD of Puccini's *La Bohème*. I loved it, but everyone else wanted to hear rock music. Anyway, it was just a friendship. I lost track of her when we all went off to college."

Silence falls over the couple as they walk. Lisa thinks of Isabella, wondering where she is now—maybe here in one of these beautiful towns they are visiting—and if she even remembers Bobby.

Bobby thinks back to the Arena di Verona, and the magical opera performance he and Lisa had been lucky to hear. *Now I understand why the arena was designated as a UNESCO World Heritage site*, he thinks. The Roman structure, built around 30 AD, has been so well preserved and restored that thousands of people can still enjoy the space today, flocking to the Verona Opera Festival summer programs from all over the world.

He squeezes Lisa's hand, glad she insisted they go there.

The very first opera, *Dafne*, tells the story of Apollo falling in love with the titular character, a nymph. Written by Ottavio Rinuccini and composed by Jacopo Peri, the opera was first performed in 1598 at the Palazzo Corsi in Florence. The opera must have made a good impression on the Medici family because, not long after, Peri's next opera, *Euridice*, was performed at the wedding of the French King Henry IV and Marie de' Medici. From that momentous beginning, Italian composers such as Verdi, Rossini, Puccini, and Monteverdi made opera popular throughout Europe and beyond.

La Scala (*Teatro alla Scala*) in Milan is perhaps the most

famous opera house in the world. The best Italian singers have performed there. It was built from 1776 to 1778, when the region was under Austrian rule, and it later served as a meeting place for traders and businessmen who negotiated their deals, even while operas were being performed.

La Scala closed during World War I, but with help from Italian conductor Arturo Toscanini, who organized benefit concerts, it reopened in 1920. It has been restored and renovated several times since then, and is now home to a ballet company, ballet school, and a singing school.

La Scala's season begins each year on December 7, the feast day of Saint Ambrose, the patron of Milan. Opening day is so important that tickets are nearly impossible to obtain.

"Which saint is looking over us now?" Bobby says, putting his arm around Lisa's waist as they walk slowly along one of Siena's narrow streets.

Their stay in Siena is short—in a few days they will drive west to Gubbio in the region of Umbria.

"*Oombria*," he says.

"*Oombria*," Lisa repeats. "I've always wanted to see it. Especially Gubbio, the medieval city with buildings five hundred years old and probably a lot older—which is just normal for Italy. And to answer your question—Saint Catherine, of course! Catherine of Siena had a vision of Jesus when she was very little. She devoted herself to helping the poor, and she organized a women's monastery right here in Siena somewhere."

"When did she live?" Bobby asks. He likes placing people and events in time.

"She was born here in Siena in 1347," Lisa says. "When she was older, she refused to let her parents marry her off. She had visions and became an influential activist—some say she had a keen mind. She wrote hundreds of letters to men in power and to simple peasants. She gave herself over to caring for the poor and people who were sick from the plague. But she fasted too often, so she died young."

"Well, thank you, Saint Catherine, for watching over our visit here to your beautiful city," Bobby says, looking at the stars dotting the dark night sky. He smiles upward and spreads out his arms, then wraps them around Lisa in a bear hug.

GUBBIO

"My name is Luca," the slim young waiter introduces himself. He sets down a bottle of Pellegrino on the small table where Bobby and Lisa sit, a map spread out before them. It's late afternoon. "Welcome to Gubbio!" he says with a flourish.

"*GOO-bio*," Bobby repeats, trying to pronounce it the way Luca did. The waiter smiles in amusement at Bobby's attempt. Gubbio, they have learned, has a population of just thirty-one thousand people.

Lisa studies the guidebook. According to legend, she reads, a wolf had been attacking the people and livestock of Gubbio, so a friar named Francis—known later as St. Francis—spoke to the animal and discovered it was only hungry. He and the townspeople fed the hungry wolf to tame it, and the town was safe once again.

Luca proudly shows off his English to his American customers. "Ah, I see your map," he says. "Here in Gubbio, you can walk to most places. We Italians like to walk. We walk to the market, to work . . . this way we see our neighbors and friends every day."

"But cars and scooters are everywhere," Lisa points out.

"*Sì, sì*, we love cars and scooters and motorcycles. But it's really best to travel by foot through our cities, villages, and along the country roads," Luca replies. "I have lived here all my life, and I have never owned a car or scooter. Take my word for it—walk around any city, and you will get to know Italy and people much more quickly, and more . . . intimately. So, what is on your itinerary today?"

"One thing for sure, we want to find some good gelato," Lisa says.

"Ah, I will give you a few tips for gelato," Luca says, leaning forward to whisper his secrets. "Beware of gelato that is, how would I say . . . bright in color. This is not natural, and you only want gelato made of natural ingredients. Also, the gelato must not be shiny—that means it was made with too much sugar. And don't go to shops that sell chips or toppings. Good gelato does not need anything extra. My tips for you." Luca winks.

Bobby and Lisa smile gratefully. They finish their Pellegrino and get up to leave, feeling glad to have been saved from inferior gelato.

"Ciao!" Luca says cheerfully, before turning to greet his next customers. "And have a beautiful walk!"

Bobby and Lisa set off on foot, taking Luca's advice. The streets are full of people enjoying the cool temperature and bright sunlight. Lisa is delighted by the sight of a black cat sitting like a king at the edge of a small fountain. Magenta geraniums spill over the edge of a large clay pot near the entrance of a low apartment building. Somewhere within, a child shouts something and a father's deep voice responds.

All of a sudden, Lisa spies a sign: GELATO. "Dare we?" she asks.

"Yes!" Bobby replies as he tries to remember Luca's advice.

They pick up the pace. Bobby grabs Lisa's hand and they smile at each other. Ten minutes later, they are walking again, holding two little cups of the sweet dessert.

Even while she eats her gelato with a pink plastic spoon, Lisa feels like they've stepped into a different century. Narrow stone pedestrian walkways branch out in every direction, leading to old stone bridges and sturdy ancient buildings. She wonders what people looked like walking on these streets hundreds of years ago, and what they would think of modern gelato flavors, of tourists from across the ocean. *If only buildings could speak*, she thinks, remembering Bobby's comment just days before. *They could tell us about the clothes, the looks of each generation who walked on these streets.*

Over the course of the day, they visited the Palazzo dei Consoli and crossed the stream that runs through the town to the very pleasant neighborhood of San Martino. At one point, they came upon Piazza Giordano Bruno and learned the story of the man it was named after, a story that reveals the prejudices of his day.

Now, while Lisa naps in a large chair in their hotel room, Bobby unpacks his iPad and tries to learn more about Friar Giordano Bruno. Born in 1548, Bruno became a Dominican friar at age seventeen. Throughout his life he was a mathematician, poet, and philosopher, writing about the techniques for memorizing texts and theorizing about the universe. Bruno suggested that space was infinite and had no central focal point, and that perhaps stars were like the sun and had their own circling planets.

These ideas got Bruno into trouble with the church, and he went on the run to avoid persecution. He found welcome in France and England. But Bruno eventually returned to Italy, where he enjoyed some celebrity status for his intellect and popular demonstrations of his memorization abilities. But he agreed with the astronomer Nicolaus Copernicus, who claimed the Earth circled the sun and not vice versa, an idea considered anti-religious. For this Bruno was hung naked, upside down in the Campo de' Fiori in Rome, then burned at the stake. He was fifty-two years old.

Upside down and naked? Burned at the stake? Bobby gulps. He glances at Lisa, whose eyes are blissfully closed, and decides to spare her the gruesome details.

He opens his map of Italy and stares at the familiar shape,

running his finger along the road they traveled to get to Gubbio. "For such a small country, Italy has an astonishing variety of landscapes," Bobby says, though he doubts Lisa is listening.

Lisa is *not* listening. Although her eyes are closed, she's thinking about all the well-dressed Italians she passes every day. What is it that makes their style so distinctive? Why exactly do Italian women—*all of them*, young and old—look so good? She decides it's not that their clothes are expensive, but that they fit their figures perfectly.

"Italy is only 113,567 square miles . . . it has so much," Bobby continues. "Beaches on the Amalfi Coast. Sicily has Mount Etna, an active volcano. I would love to see that when it's covered in snow."

"The lakes up north, don't forget them—I want to see Lake Como and all the colorful homes and elegant hotels along the water's edge," Lisa murmurs.

"Italy may be small, but it's so full of beauty, it seems like there is always more to see and explore," Bobby says. "Well over four thousand miles of coastline, a thousand lakes, the islands of Capri, Sardinia, and Sicily, and the Alps and the Dolomites . . . I guess we have plenty to see on our next trip."

"It's so interesting—Italians live in a harmonious coexistence with natural beauty," Lisa says, now fully awake and reflecting philosophically. "They live in hilltop towns, in little villages by the water, and in cities built up and around Roman ruins, medieval churches, mountains, and lakes. Most people would just tear down all the ancient buildings, but Italians work with them and preserve them."

"You're right," Bobby says. "Instead of leveling the landscapes, they work around them. Because they respect their country's treasures, they find ways to live among them."

"Well, it's to their benefit," Lisa says. "People come from all over the world to see these treasures."

"It says here that Italy boasts *fifty-eight* UNESCO Heritage Sites, topping all other countries. I'm not surprised—are you?"

PERUGIA

"Lisa, can you *hurry it up?*"

Bobby is eager to leave the hotel, but Lisa has been combing her hair, twisting it on top of her head, then changing her mind and letting it fall.

"Okay, just one more minute," she says.

Bobby sighs. "I really want go to Piazza Italia tonight." He's starving. Having arrived in Perugia earlier in the day, they had explored the charming medieval town, working up a thirst and an appetite.

"Why, what's there?" Lisa is curious.

"Well, you said you like to listen, right?" Lisa nods. "In the old section of Perugia, if you stand in one spot near the arches and I stand diagonally opposite, I should be able to hear whatever you say, even if you whisper."

"How does that happen?" Lisa asks.

"It's the way it was designed. Are you ready to go?"

"Yes—let's figure out where we can eat afterward," Lisa says, grabbing her sweater as they head out.

It is still early evening and the air is cool. From every direction they hear the pleasant sounds of people talking and laughing. They pass crowds of young people along the Corso Vannucci. As a city with two universities, Perugia's streets are filled with students at all hours.

Bobby and Lisa come to the Piazza IV Novembre. In the center is a large round fountain, Fontana Maggiore, with carved panels.

The faint lilting of an accordion drifts toward them. They turn a corner, and there he is—a young musician sitting on a box at the intersection of two wide streets, eyes closed as he plays. His cap is placed upside down on the ground in front of him for donations.

Lisa smiles and stops to enjoy his song. Accordion music makes life feel so joyful. The moments elongate with every impressive, harmonious range of sounds he draws out, as if each one is a great, deep breath.

The Accordion Story

Accordions are complex instruments. They are hand-crafted by necessity; each one requires about six thousand pieces. A town called Castelfidardo in central eastern Italy is famous for its top accordion manufacturers. For more than a century, Castelfidardo craftsmen have made some of the world's finest accordions.

Paolo Soprani, one of the town's most well-known accordion manufacturers, first moved there in 1872 to open a small shop, and his accordions became increasingly popular. As Italians began emigrating to other countries, they ordered the instruments to be sent to them so they could play the familiar music in their new homes.

Excuse me, I need to say something—I love accordions, and I'm not surprised they are made here in Italy. Italians know how to use our hands to make many complicated and beautiful objects.

Italians have *pazienza*—patience. This is very important, and I am afraid in this fast, modern world, nobody has that anymore. Everything has to be *molto veloce*!

But listen—these masters, maybe they have education, maybe they don't. But they can work on these accordions, making them just right, so musicians can play the happiest music in the world. What a gift, eh?

Here, listen to what the writer is saying . . .

Pigini, a large accordion manufacturer in Castelfidardo today, was started by Filippo Pigini in 1946. Pigini makes more than two hundred models of accordions and ships them around the world. The company makes almost all its accordion parts in-house.

Yet another big name in the accordion world is Gianfranco

Gabbanelli, though his company is not in Castelfidardo. Gabbanelli came to the US from Italy in 1961 and began making and selling accordions just as he'd learned to do in Italy. He taught his son, Mike, about making accordions, and today Mike runs the company with the help of a team of Italian artisans and tuners, maintaining a high standard of quality in their instruments.

City of Violins

Hours later, after a delicious dinner of pappardelle with a thick ragù, warm bread, and *gnocconi* with fresh ricotta, Lisa and Bobby wander back to their hotel. They stop to look into shop windows and peek into restaurants with outdoor patios strung with lights, where diners focus on conversation over plates of delicious-looking food. Wineglasses clink for a toast, followed by happy laughter.

But Lisa has turned her head in another direction. Bobby notices the light glinting on her hair. "What's that music?" she asks.

Up ahead they spot a petite young woman standing at the corner of a piazza. She is playing a familiar Vivaldi melody from *The Four Seasons* on her violin. On the front of her bright purple T-shirt are the words CONSERVATORIO DI MILANO. Propped up on the ground nearby is a handwritten sign asking for coins. Lisa and Bobby stop, mesmerized by the lovely melody.

After she finishes and takes a bow, Lisa approaches tentatively. "Your music is beautiful!" she remarks.

"Thank you," the young violinist replies. "You are a musician too?" Though she is Italian, she speaks English perfectly. Her curly brown hair is pulled back in a thick ponytail.

"No, no, not at all. We are music lovers, though," Lisa says. She points to the young woman's shirt. "Are you a student at the Milan Conservatory?"

"*Sì*. I have been there one year. But I like to play outdoors for people passing by, who come from different countries."

Lisa smiles and studies the dark orange surface of her violin. It looks ancient. The violinist's eyes light up when she sees Lisa's admiration, and she enthusiastically explains. "Do you know Cremona? It's a small city north of Milano in the Po Valley. For musicians throughout the world, Cremona is famous. It's where handcrafted violins are made, a tradition dating back hundreds of years."

"Wow, I didn't know that . . ." Lisa says, suddenly feeling ignorant.

"Cremona is where the first Stradivarius was made," the young musician states with pride. She smiles and steps back to play again for the passersby. Bobby and Lisa drop several euros in her donation box, then continue their walk.

"Don't you wonder what they do in Cremona? I mean, what is it that makes those violins so special?" Lisa ponders aloud.

When they get back to their hotel that night, Bobby uses his iPad to research more about Cremona. "Listen to this," he says. "Violin-maker Philippe Devanneaux once said, 'Of course, you can make a violin with a machine or a computer, but you can't put your heart inside of it.' Doesn't that sound very Italian?"

"Yes," Lisa agrees. "If something can be made by hand, Italians have probably been doing it for hundreds of years."

"About six hundred years ago, artists flourished in Cremona," Bobby says. "Andrea Amati is credited as the maker of the first violin. In his lifetime—from 1505 to 1577—he made approximately thirty-six violins, primarily for royalty. Then his sons carried on the tradition, and Amati's grandson Nicolò took a teen apprentice named Antonio Stradivari, who grew up to establish his own family workshop. Another famous violin maker—'luthier' is actually the correct term—was Joseph Guarnerius del Gesù, born in Cremona in 1698, who was influenced by Stradivari."

Lisa is glad Bobby likes to do this research. She stops brushing her teeth to listen to him.

"Cremona was in the news recently. Sound experts have recorded musicians playing the oldest, most fragile violins. Everyone worried the original violins will deteriorate, so three sound engineers, along with leaders of Cremona's Museo del Violino, digitally recorded the oldest violins and cellos so future generations will be able to hear them while they are still playable. They invited top musicians to Cremona to play two violins, a viola, and a cello. They discovered, though, that the ultrasensitive recording equipment they were using picked up all the little noises of everyday Cremona life outside the recording studio."

"Oh, no! How did they solve that problem?"

"They asked Cremona's residents to be as quiet as possible during the hours of recording. No honking horns, no Vespas, no breaking glass, no knocking on doors, and no shouts of '*Buongiorno!*' And they did it."

"Wow," Lisa exclaims, "Italians *really* care about preservation."

"Maybe we can visit Cremona one day," Bobby muses. "I would love to see the workshops and meet the violin-makers. You know, these violins are still the most sought-after instruments in the world."

"I'm going to dream about violin music now," Lisa says as she pulls up the covers. Exhausted by a long day of sightseeing, she immediately falls asleep.

ASSISI

We are now in Assisi and music, singers, instruments . . . all things musical are held in very high regard by Italians. I've noticed little sounds help me understand the Italian sensibilities and ways of life. When I take a few moments to listen, really pay attention—like right now—this is what I hear . . .

Lisa writes in the travel journal she's kept with her on this trip. Sitting up in bed as the morning sun peeks through the thin white curtains, she begins to write. She turns her head toward the tall window of their hotel room, which they'd left partially open. She lists sounds from the street below and what they are teaching her:

1. *Two women are talking to each other cheerfully from their windows—communities are important in Italy.*

2. A man is singing while he sweeps in front of a store—singing makes work easier.

3. A Vespa, or some kind of scooter, is speeding down an alley nearby—young people are on the move!

She sighs—it's just a typical morning in Assisi.

Bobby sleeps soundly by her side, but she is eager to get out and explore. She gives him a little shove and he opens his eyes.

"*Buongiorno, amore mio*," she says.

"There is only one sound I love hearing more than you speaking Italian," he says, blinking his eyes at her in the morning sun.

"And that is . . . ?"

"The sound of Italian coffee being brewed," Bobby replies. They laugh and jump out of bed to go find some.

Scooters

Two motor scooters buzz in tandem up the street. The young man and woman driving them call out to each other playfully.

"Looks fun, doesn't it?" Bobby says. He holds up a brochure about renting a scooter for the day as he and Lisa enter a bar near the Piazza del Comune.

"*Buongiorno, cosa desidera?*" a middle-aged waiter asks Bobby.

"*Due caffè, per favore*," Bobby replies. To Lisa, he says, "Hey, I just answered him in Italian without even thinking!"

"I think this scooter adventure is all yours," Lisa teases.

"If you change your mind, I found out you can even take a tour by Vespa. One company provides a four-hour tour called 'Rome Movie Sets' that includes visits to the sites where *Roman Holiday*, *Angels & Demons*, *Ben Hur*, and *La Dolce Vita*, the Federico Fellini film, were shot."

"I'd rather visit Piazza del Comune and the Basilica di San Francesco. Do you even know the Saint Francis prayer?" Lisa asks.

Bobby nods, but he's focused on the brochure.

"'Lord, make me an instrument of your peace,'" Lisa begins. "'Where there is hatred, let me sow love. Where there is injury, pardon. Where there is doubt, faith . . .'"

"It's really okay with you if I do this?" Bobby breaks in, not hearing her recite the famous prayer. He's too focused on reading in the brochure all the places where he can rent a scooter for the day.

The waiter brings two small cups of coffee.

"Yes, of course." Lisa smiles. "It seems like the ultimate Italian thing to do, but I don't want to join you."

Bobby picks up his coffee cup and inhales the intense aroma. "You know my aunt Kathe in Boston? She once told me a story about a Vespa. When she was seventeen, she visited Rome to spend the summer with her own aunt and uncle. By chance, she met a charming Italian boy named Carlo, who was also seventeen. He offered to give Kathe a tour of Rome on the back of his pale green Vespa. Her aunt and uncle disapproved, but off Kathe went."

"Oh, how romantic!" Lisa says.

"As she described the experience, it was heaven. To be riding with this cool guy on this beautifully designed machine—it was the perfect way to see Rome," Bobby continues.

"Carlo took her to see all the main attractions, and the next day, he showed up on his Vespa again. That day he took her to Tivoli to meet his extended family for Sunday lunch. They ate plate after plate of food. No one spoke English and Aunt Kathe didn't speak Italian, but she said no translation was needed. Carlo's family just welcomed her as a friend of their son's."

"What a great memory!" Lisa says. "I bet every time she hears the buzzing of a scooter she remembers riding on the Vespa with Carlo."

"Are you sure you don't want to go with me today?"

"I'm sure—I also want to see the Basilica di Santa Chiara. You know Saint Clare? She was a friend of Saint Francis *and* joined his order, which was a shocking thing for a woman. The church has a crucifix that spoke to Saint Francis—that's the legend, anyway."

"Let me know if it tells *you* anything, such as where we should eat dinner tonight."

"Don't be irreverent!" Lisa says, then kisses her husband. "Have fun today!"

It's me, Nina, *mi scusi, per favore.* I want to say that I remember when the Vespa first came out—oh, what a big thing it was, especially for the young people.

Dear reader, I know you want to find out about Bobby's Vespa adventure, but I can tell you, kids on the Vespa— imagine how their parents felt! I was already a mother, so it wasn't for me to hop on one of those, but I envied the boys and girls who did.

My little cousin Mina had a boyfriend who somehow got a Vespa and he would come around to pick up Mina after dinner. She was one of seven kids, so it took a few hours for her mother to notice one of her daughters was not in the house. And where was she? Her sisters told their mother, *Oh, Mina went to her friend's house. She'll be back soon.* They wanted Mina to have fun on the Vespa. It was pale green too, not like any color we'd seen.

If he hadn't had that Vespa, would she have loved him? I don't think so.

Bobby sits astride the baby blue Vespa he has rented for the day. He is barely able to contain his excitement. He's ridden them back home, so he understands how scooters maneuver. After briefly looking at a map, he revs the motor and takes off down the narrow street. Before he knows it, he has left Assisi heading south, surrounded by Umbria's rolling green hills. He feels magnificently free with the wind against his face and the clear sky ahead. All of life is good, pure, exciting.

But . . . where is he going? Without Lisa by his side, he feels strangely lost.

Dear reader, I must break in here again. I used to like going to the movies—so much fun! If you are from my generation, do you remember *Roman Holiday*? When I was young, I secretly wanted a Vespa, or at least to drive one myself—but women were not allowed.

Yet, in the movie, lovely Audrey Hepburn was a free-thinking princess longing to experience life. Gregory Peck played the charming newspaperman who falls in love with her. Ah, what a movie! *Molto romantico!*

The writer wants to explain . . .

Roman Holiday was the movie that made the scooter famous. In some of the finest scenes, the two stars careen around Rome holding on to each other and their Vespa for dear life, defying all social rules by falling in love. This movie launched Vespa scooters into world fame.

After World War II, who could afford a car? The scooter was the answer. Emilio Piaggio invented the Vespa in the late 1940s. The vehicles became so popular that Piaggio built a while line of them, including Vespas just for racing. By the time *Roman Holiday* came out in 1953, the Vespa was the way to travel for fun-loving boys and girls. It was an expression of Italy's joy of living from the moment it was invented.

Bobby sees a sign for the city of Todi and realizes he's been motoring on the Vespa for about thirty miles. He slows down and navigates the crowded stone streets to the center of Todi. *Scooters may not reach high speeds, but they are perfect for these little lanes*, he thinks.

He parks the Vespa and walks to the main square. He stops—the view makes him gasp. Rolling hills dotted with ancient stone buildings stretch out below him, as if from a fairy tale. Flowers in clay pots adorn windowsills and doorways of the surrounding streets and alleys. A cool breeze wafts through the square, and children's laughter spills out from a walled school play yard.

Suddenly, he aches for Lisa. He wishes she could see—and hear!—all of this. "*Ooom-bria*," he mutters to himself, starting back on the road to Assisi.

Speaking Italian

"Italians love to talk," Bobby says, watching three men standing on the corner of a park in spirited conversation.

"And I love listening to them," Lisa says. She and Bobby cross a cobblestone street in Assisi, passing the three men, who do not stop to even glance at them.

Following Bobby's day on the Vespa, he and Lisa decide to visit the Basilica di San Francesco, just outside Assisi. "The basilica's lower church is dark and moody," Lisa comments as they approach the hill. "And there is a place called the Hill of Hell, where they used to execute people."

"Lovely," Bobby says with good humor. But he is impressed by the church. As they pass through the somber lower church space, they admire the colorful frescoes.

Saint Francis, who lived a life of poverty, is an important figure in history—many people emulated his selflessness and care for animals. His resting place is a major destination for Catholics around the world. The basilica was built soon after his death in 1226.

Bobby and Lisa move into the upper church and stare up at the soaring height of the ceiling, covered with paintings. They find the twenty-eight-part fresco *The Life of Saint Francis*, painted primarily by Giotto di Bondone, depicting highlights of the saint's life, such as the moment a crucifix spoke to him and the day he gave up all his possessions.

A small group of Italian teenagers is corralled by a young woman, clearly their art teacher. She points to the fresco and speaks to them in rapid Italian—too fast for Bobby to even catch one word.

"The Italian language is so melodious and musical, full of ups and downs and flourishes," Lisa whispers.

"I've heard English, French, German, Mandarin, Japanese, and even Swedish in all the places we've been in Italy so far," Bobby says. "I'm sure after the foreigners all go home, we'd hear only Italian."

"I love how enthusiastically Italians curse. Remember when we took that taxi ride in Florence and the driver was cussing at the bicyclist in his way? I understood his meaning quite well!" They both laughed at the memory of the driver shaking his fist and the bicyclist responding with an equally rude gesture.

"My goal is to learn the proper pronunciations," Bobby says. "Right now we are in *Ah-SEE-zee*. The accent is always on an unexpected syllable—or unexpected to me, anyway. And then there is the combination of long and short consonants. And you're supposed to linger on some consonants to extend them."

"What do you mean?" Lisa asks.

"Well, to say *La Nona di Beethoven*, or Beethoven's Ninth Symphony, is quite different from *La Nonna di Beethoven*, which means 'Beethoven's grandmother.'"

"Oh, I see," Lisa says. "Italian has a little lift to each word. Even when they are speaking other languages, Italians can't help but add that flourish. It's so endearing."

"I once read a quote from Charles V, who lived in the 1500s," Bobby remembers. "It goes something like this: 'I speak Spanish to God, Italian to women, French to men, and German to my horse.'" Lisa laughs.

SPOLETO

"Let's see . . . we heard opera and jazz, and we saw a ballet and two plays. I think we walked all over Spoleto," Lisa says.

She and Bobby planned their trip so they could be in Spoleto for its famous annual summer music event, Festival dei Due Mondi, or the Festival of Two Worlds. Dance performances, art exhibits, and music of all kinds comprise the program, filling every indoor and outdoor venue in town. And in their off-hours, artists, dancers, and musicians enjoyed Spoleto as much as the tourists. In 1958, the founder, Gian Carlo Menotti, hoped it would be a meeting of American and European cultures. Today, America holds its counterpart, the Spoleto Festival USA, in Charleston, South Carolina, every year.

Now the Spoleto festival has ended, and Bobby and Lisa sip espressos in a crowded bistro and talk about their favorite festival moments.

"What a concentration of talent!" Lisa says, thinking about the art and performers from hundreds of countries who had enthralled them in this hilltop town for ten days.

"Even if there had been no festival here, I would love this little town," Bobby says. "The Cattedrale di Santa Maria Assunta is so elegant." As he lifts a tiny espresso cup to his mouth, he pauses. His eyes scan the horizon outside. "Listen . . ." he says, but Lisa only hears the peal of church bells in the distance. "It's such an ancient, soulful sound. It's meant to tell everyone the time or to remind us to pray, but it feels like a reminder that this is an old village, that humanity has been here for centuries, that we are all the same. Remember when we heard the church bells in Venice for that wedding?"

Lisa smiles. She loves Bobby's romantic side. He often has these kinds of philosophical moments. She reaches over to run her fingers through his hair. "Well, it also has something to do with the fact that Italy is a Catholic country," she says. "Why don't we explore churches today?"

Mi scusi, I have to ask, what is so surprising about the church bells ringing? The tourists all stop and listen as if they've never heard church bells before.

Oh, this is Nina interrupting again, but by now you are used to me!

Somebody told me that Italy has sixty-seven thousand churches. Their bells ring to mark the hours, half hours, and sometimes even quarter hours. When I was growing up, church bells would ring to celebrate happy occasions, like a wedding, or sad ones, like a funeral.

The sound is *molto familiare*—it comforts me. I am very sorry for anyone who didn't have church bells in their child-hoods. That's what I wanted to tell you.

But look at Bobby and Lisa now—they've arrived in Roma!

ROME

"What is the one sound we've heard in nearly every town and village and city in Italy?" Lisa quizzes Bobby.

"Wine being poured?"

"No. Well, yes, but—"

"The sound of people laughing and eating dinner late into the night?" he tries again.

"I was thinking of the bubbling water in all the fountains," Lisa says. "It is such a soothing sound, and I hear it everywhere."

She and Bobby arrived in Rome by train the day before. She had spotted one of the city's cast-iron public drinking fountains in the corner of a small piazza almost immediately. A simple spigot, she watched men and women stop there to fill a water bottle or simply lean down to take a drink. Called *nasone*—the spigot's shape is similar to a nose—about 2,500 of these drinking fountains are publicly accessible and very helpful on hot summer days. After noticing one or two, you will observe how many ordinary Romans stop to enjoy this cold, refreshing water that is safe for all to drink.

"Everywhere we go, I hear the bubbling water from all the fountains," Lisa says. "It's a peaceful noise that muffles the traffic sounds."

They are headed toward the marble Trevi Fountain—"*Fontana di TREV-ee*," Bobby says. He takes note of the city's sights and sounds: the honking horns from buses; clanging bells from street cars coursing along embedded tracks; the slow-moving Tiber River; the ancient stone bridges and ruins that appear suddenly; huge white marble monuments honoring leaders in Italian history, looming over open squares; charming small restaurants with open doors, their tables covered in fresh white tablecloths.

It's late afternoon as they head to the Piazza di Trevi. Turning a corner, it pops into view—the huge fountain standing 86 feet high and 161 feet long, surrounded by visitors and admirers, as if it were a kind of shrine. Transfixed by the scene, with the rush of fountain water filling the air, Lisa and Bobby stare for a moment.

"That sound . . . it's like the Mediterranean waves lapping on the shore, or rain falling," Lisa says.

The massive Trevi Fountain was built at the end of an ancient aqueduct at an intersection of three streets, hence the name: *tre vie*. Designed by architect Nicholas Salvi and completed in about 1762, the fountain features the nearly naked god Neptune standing on a chariot shaped as a shell, drawn by wild horses.

Since then, the Trevi Fountain has achieved worldwide celebrity status. It appeared in the 1954 movie *Three Coins in the Fountain* and then in the 1960 film *La Dolce Vita* by Federico Fellini, in which Marcello Mastroianni and Anita Ekberg frolic in the fountain together at night.

The sun sets, shadows take over, street lights come on, and the nightlife begins.

Lisa sighs and leans her head on Bobby's shoulder. "I would not want to be anywhere else in the world with anyone else but you."

Bobby kisses her. "That's good, because I feel the very same way."

They turn to walk back toward their hotel.

"Don't forget," he adds, "we will be coming back to Rome at the end of our trip—and we planned on four days here, right?"

"Yes, and even that will be hardly enough to see it all . . ." Lisa sighs.

Mega Fountains of Tivoli

Intrigued by the fountains, Lisa stays up late that night in the hotel reading about them on Bobby's iPad. He snores, but she is wide awake.

The most imaginative fountains in the world, she reads, surround the Villa d'Este in Tivoli, built during the Renaissance period for Cardinal Ippolito d'Este, who lived from 1509 to 1572. His gardens and fountains are like a Renaissance Disneyland. The cardinal poured huge amounts of money into creating his expansive gardens in order to impress men of influence and to prove his power and might. Like other cardinals in his time, he was angling to be named pope, the most powerful position in the world—and wildly imaginative gardens were a way of making a good impression. In doing so, he went into debt. Though d'Este never did become pope, his villa and gardens are a testament to his sense of drama and playfulness—and have been designated as a UNESCO World Heritage site.

The elaborate gardens were built from 1566 to 1577—they took more than twenty years to complete—with design help from Pirro Ligorio, an architect, landscaper, and painter who was very interested in Roman antiquities. The dramatic water features he planned for the cardinal's garden required two aqueducts, which diverted water from nearby rivers. Antique statues were lugged over from the villa of Roman emperor Hadrian, and new ones were carved depicting animals, plants, and mythological figures—some dignified, others comical.

Incredibly, the fountains operated—then and now—*without* pumps. The vast green garden's fountains, falls, jets, pools, canals, and more demonstrate masterful hydraulic engineering. The Hundred Fountains, for example, features water spouting out of the mouths of two long rows of animal-like stone masks, with additional jets spraying water into the air one level above.

Another extravagant feature of the Villa d'Este garden is a mini replica of Rome. The story goes that when the pope told Cardinal d'Este he could not build his own palace in Rome, d'Este angrily responded by building this miniature city on the grounds of his Tivoli garden, showing that he "owned" Rome.

But the garden's most spectacular engineering feat is the Fountain of the Organ, with waterways and pipes built to play music. Powered by pressure—again, no pumps!—the water forces a wheel to turn, opening valves for more than twenty pipes. As the water forces air up through these pipes, it causes them to play music. The pipes "play" four pieces of Renaissance music every two hours.

Lisa looks up directions to Cardinal d'Este's villa and gardens and sees they are just a forty-minute drive northeast from Rome. Excited for this next stop on their journey, she powers down the iPad, turns out the light, and settles into the fluffy hotel comforters, immediately falling asleep.

"Sei ubriaco!" *a woman shouts.* "You're drunk!"

"You're right, I am!"

Lisa turns and sees the actress Anita Ekberg shouting at Marcello Mastroianni. She and Bobby are standing with the actors in the middle of the Trevi Fountain, their fine evening clothes soaking wet.

"Sì, è vero." *Marcello throws his head back and laughs heartily.*

Anita starts splashing Marcello, getting his elegant black suit even wetter. A bright full moon glows in the sky above them. Bobby also wears a black suit, and Lisa cannot help but start splashing him too. He turns and laughs, then falls backward. When he stands up, water pours down his face.

Lisa laughs, and the others laugh too. Just then, a police siren sounds. Are we allowed to be in this famous fountain? *Lisa worries. She tries to dash for the edge of the fountain, but she can't move. Suddenly, Marcello bursts into song and Anita joins in, both swaying in drunken happiness as the siren grows louder.*

Bobby grabs Lisa's hand and says, "Don't worry. If we are arrested, it will be another amazing Italian experience . . ."

Lisa awakes with a jolt.

She is not in the Trevi Fountain after all, but in bed with Bobby, who is snoring contentedly, as usual. She turns and closes her eyes again, glad she doesn't have to go to jail.

Touch

THE FEEL OF LUXURY

NAPLES

After their Rome adventures, Bobby and Lisa arrive in Naples.

"Have you ever run your fingers over Italian silk?" Lisa asks.

But she already knows the answer. In Naples, much of Italy's finest clothing is manufactured. But that doesn't mean much to Bobby.

"Umm, no," Bobby says. "Have I been missing something?" He doesn't share her interest in fashion.

"Yes! It's sublime, perfect, super soft . . ." she says dreamily. "It's all part of the famous quality of Italian style." She ponders for the hundredth time why Italians look so good. *Is it simply that their fabrics are better quality?* "Italians dress well no matter where they are going. Style almost seems to be a cultural tradition. It's not about wealth, it's about self-esteem. Italians take a lot of pride in how they look—they want to present well, and they do."

The couple sits at a table just off Via dei Tribunali, an ideal spot from which to study the style of dress in the passersby. Having just finished a full lunch, Lisa and Bobby sit back and enjoy the scene.

"*NAH-polee*," Bobby likes to say, practicing the correct pronunciation. The city is big and congested, but the street in front of the restaurant is set off from the wider boulevards and is lined with palm trees. Fast-walking, stylish Italians stream past their table, delighting Lisa.

Bobby, watching idly, drinks a glass of Pellegrino. Suddenly, he sits up straight. An older couple juggle their guidebooks while attempting to open a map. The man looks lost, even glancing up at the sky as if searching for some sign of which way to go. His wife puts on glasses and peers down at the map. "Stop!" Bobby shouts. "Thief—*ladro!*" A man in tight jeans and a sweatshirt is reaching inside the woman's bag, but freezes with his hand on her wallet. The woman and her husband turn and realize what is happening. "Thief! Stop him!" they call out. A nearby pair of *Carabinieri* chase after the thief as he races away down an alley.

"Thank you," the woman says to Bobby, revealing a British accent. "He dropped my wallet, thankfully."

"We were told to beware of pickpockets, but we are just not used to that," her husband says, shaking his head as his wife zippers her bag shut. The couple are wearing nearly matching tweed jackets.

"Well, Napoli is a big city, so I suppose it's to be expected," Bobby says. "I'm glad you are all right."

"We've loved Naples so far," the woman says. "We've just been over to the seafront—Santa Lucia. It's gorgeous! And the Castel dell'Ovo is enchanting. Do you know the story of Virgil placing an egg under its foundation? It was said that when the egg breaks, there will be a great disaster here."

"It's probably broken to bits by now," the man chuckles. "How long have you been here in Naples?"

"Just a few days," Lisa says. "The climate is warmer, and Naples is a little grittier than most northern cities we've been to. But everyone has been very friendly."

"And it has so much great architecture," Bobby adds.

"If you like architecture, you must see Piazza del Plebiscito, the Peoples' Plaza. It's magnificent. A huge arc of open space, with elegant buildings all around the edge, including the Royal Palace—lots of rooms fit for the royals of Naples."

"And another thing you must do," the woman adds, "is taste the famous pizza. It really is different here than anywhere else—and very good!"

"We must be on our way, dear," the man says. "Thank you again for averting a disaster!" he says to Bobby before the pair toddle off together.

Lisa and Bobby wave goodbye, pay the bill for lunch, and turn to walk toward the water.

"I want to find Chiaia, the neighborhood *and* the street," Lisa says, knowing it's nearby.

"*Vee-ya kee-EYE-ya,*" Bobby says.

As they walk, Lisa continues studying Italian style. *Their hair is neat. Their shoes are polished. And their clothes are simple but very well made*, she reflects. "Italian fabrics—cotton, wool, and silk—you can feel the quality when you touch it," she says.

A young woman walks by wearing a green dress and carrying a bright pink handbag. "Italians really do have a flair for creativity," Bobby comments.

"Versace, Cerruti, Ferragamo, Armani, Prada . . . Italian designers change the way people think about style," Lisa says. "The whole world follows their lead."

She glances down at Bobby's old running shoes and grimaces. He notices this and stiffens. *Is she judging my clothes again?* he wonders.

The Eccentric Genius of Elsa Schiaparelli

In trying to understand Italian fashion, Lisa has learned a bit of its history. And she's discovered one woman she admires very much: the most glamorous and unusual Elsa Schiaparelli. Her styles could be called eccentric, or simply creative and fun. She was famous for her "speakeasy dress"—a fringed gown with a hidden pocket just big enough to hold a flask—and hat in the shape of an upside-down shoe.

Elsa was as savvy about finances as she was in design. When times were economically tight in Europe during World War II, Schiaparelli was the first to use a new, smooth-to-the-touch material called rayon, a semi-synthetic fabric.

Schiaparelli—or Schiap, as she was affectionately

called—was born in Rome to an aristocratic family in 1890, and she rebelled from early age. At twenty-one, she published a collection of sensual poems, which resulted in her parents packing her off to a convent in Switzerland. She escaped to work in London, where she married and had a daughter. She later divorced and took her daughter to Paris so they could live among artists and intellectuals—free-thinking people who valued creativity and imagination.

Pablo Picasso, Salvador Dali, and Jean Cocteau were among her friends, and Schiap expressed her own artistic talents in her clothing design: a white organdy evening gown with a red lobster painted on the front; a dark blue jacket with zodiac signs and planets embroidered in gold thread; a necklace of large colorful insects marching in a circle. During Prohibition in New York, her speakeasy dress was a huge hit, becoming known as "jazz-age fashion." She also created see-through raincoats, as well as wrap dresses, which were daring for her time.

Texture was as important as design, and Schiap used rayon when natural fabrics were too costly. She experimented with making blends of natural and man-made fabrics that imitated the look and feel of silk, wool, and even linen. Pleasing textures were never sacrificed.

Schiap had an uncanny ability to predict trends. Her styles were conceptual and fun, but also practical and wearable for the average women. In 1932, *Vogue* magazine called Elsa Schiaparelli one of the greatest designers of all time. Her clothing was worn by actresses such as Greta Garbo, Katharine Hepburn, and Lauren Bacall, as well as socialites, models, and royalty.

Elsa's constant travel came under suspicion during World War II when several countries, including the US, investigated her as possible spy, an accusation she worked hard to dispel.

Today, rayon is common in fashion. Thanks for this goes to Elsa Schiaparelli.

Silk Stories

"'While Elsa Schiaparelli was discovering rayon in 1929, Italian silk was a profitable export because its fine quality was—and is—known throughout the world,'" Bobby reads aloud from a book when he and Lisa reach Via Chiaia.

"I know all about Elsa Schiaparelli, so you can stop right there," Lisa scolds. Bobby's constant reading is bothering her again. "Look at this place—it is absolutely posh!" She is thrilled to see the storefront windows filled with luxury clothing. They stop in front of one.

"By the way, who is the patron saint of Naples?" Bobby teases. "And was he well-dressed?"

Lisa laughs. "Oh, Bobby, Saint Januarius, of course—otherwise known as San Gennaro. I've heard believers gather right here in Naples to watch a tiny sample of his blood turn from solid to liquid—a miracle."

Bobby looks at her skeptically. "I've been in Little Italy in New York during the San Gennaro festival. It was lots of fun, but I didn't see blood . . ."

"Little Italy is where a lot of immigrants from Naples settled when they came to America," Lisa says, starting to walk again, slowly. Bobby sees a shop of women's clothing ahead—he knows what is coming.

"You know, I do love silk . . ." Lisa says, pulling his arm. "Let's go in this shop, just for a minute."

Bobby sighs. "A minute" for Lisa really means twenty, or longer. He follows her into the boutique and pulls a guidebook from his bag to read as she shops.

Lisa admires the merchandise as a well-dressed middle-aged saleswoman stands politely nearby. At a table covered with neat stacks of silk scarves, Lisa gently picks one up, moved by its softness.

"'One center of Italian silk production is the string of picturesque towns that dot the shores of Lake Como,'" Bobby reads to her. "Okay if I read a little more to you? I think you will be interested."

"All right . . ." Lisa says. In spite of herself, she *is* interested.

"'It all began when Ludovico Sforza, the duke of Milan, planted mulberry trees around Lake Como in 1400. This was for the silkworms, which feed on them,'" he reads. "'Over time, the making of silk expanded and became a big industry. It eventually led to today's silk brands like Mantero, Clerici, and Ratti . . .'"

By now, Lisa has tuned him out. She's picked out a blue and white scarf. Holding it to her neck, she looks in a mirror to see how it looks with her red hair. She decides it makes her look very Italian.

Lisa nods to the saleswoman. "I'm sorry, I don't speak Italian, but I would like to buy this—how much is it?" she asks.

The saleswoman replies in perfect English, then adds, "Silk

is a truly sensual experience, isn't it? And best of all, you bring it back home and enjoy a little piece of Italy forever."

The Pucci Dress

Io ricordo, sì, sì. Do you see Lisa buying that silk scarf? So pretty, don't you agree?

I remember, oh, how I remember . . . The 1960s, when the silk dress all the young women wanted was one of those with swirls of color designed by a Florentine. What was his name? Ah, yes, it was Emilio Pucci. All the movie stars wanted his dresses, his pants, all with those crazy colors. It was new, modern, and very *Italiano!*

Here, I will let the writer tell that story.

The Pucci silk dress was instantly popular. The swirling pattern of color matched the rebellious, free-wheeling sensibility of the time. Pucci's colorful dresses, pants, and scarves signaled carefree fun and imagination—and because they were made with fine silk, they also felt light and luxurious.

Pucci lived through a tumultuous time in Italian history. Born in 1914 in Naples into an old noble family, he lived in the Pucci Palace in Florence for most of his life.

He was an athlete—he swam, fenced, raced cars, and skied—and was part of the 1932 Italian Olympic ski team. In 1937, he was given a full scholarship to Reed College in the US with the promise that he would establish a ski team there. He did that, and more—he designed the team's uniform. After college, he returned to Italy to become a torpedo bomber in World War II, then tried to aid in the escape of Benito Mussolini's daughter—and was caught and tortured by the gestapo. He later escaped to Switzerland.

A photographer from *Harper's Bazaar* took pictures of Pucci on the ski slopes several years later wearing tight-fitting clothing custom-made with stretch fabric. Pucci was soon hounded by manufacturers who wanted to reproduce this look. He turned them down, instead going into business for himself. He was among the first ever to produce clothing with this fabric. Pucci began with a line of sportswear, then added other items such as brightly colored silk scarves and dresses with the swirling kaleidoscope pattern, featuring up to sixteen colors.

Pucci's silk dresses became *the* look in the 1960s. Jacqueline Kennedy Onassis wore his dresses, as did Elizabeth Taylor and other celebrities. The designer's influence was also political; he served two terms in the Italian Chamber of Deputies. By the early 1990s, Pucci had expanded his brand to sheets, towels, and jewelry when his iconic dresses from the '60s became suddenly hip again, much to his delight. He died in 1992.

Shirts and Suits

Bobby paces the hotel room.

For the first time in his life, he is self-conscious of his baggy khaki shorts and running shoes. He can't help but notice the style of Italian men, how they dress with care—and they look sharp. He runs his fingers through his dark hair and wonders what to do.

That afternoon, while Lisa takes a nap—her silk purchase spread across the bed—he steps out for a walk in Naples by himself. First, he stops into an espresso bar.

Lisa is right—their shirts are such fine quality, he muses. *And their shoes—well, Italian shoes are world-famous for quality.* He feels a pang of embarrassment, suddenly aware that he must really stand out as an American here. He isn't sure he likes that.

Bobby pays for his espresso and walks back toward Via Chiaia. As he approaches the window of a men's clothing shop, he slows down to gaze into the display. The dress shirt on the mannequin looks ultra-soft. And that wool suit? He can see even from a few feet away that it would be smooth to the touch.

Could I wear these kinds of clothes? Bobby is tempted. He looks around to see if anyone notices, then steps into the shop.

An older salesman approaches. "Good afternoon. May I help you?" he says in English. Bobby notices the man is wearing a fine wool suit that fits him perfectly.

"I am just looking . . ." Bobby stammers. Then he asks, "The suit in the window, the wool is so fine—where does it come from?"

"The sheep of Italy!" the salesman replies with a broad smile. "Come, look."

He brings Bobby over to a small rack holding a selection of dark suits. "Such refined textures are the result of craftsmanship passed down through generations of textile producers," he says.

"Lanificio Bottoli, for instance, is a wool mill in Vittorio Veneto, near Venice, that has operated for more than a century and a half."

"Amazing!" Bobby says. Now that he might learn a little history, his shyness disappears.

"Would you like to try on one of these suits?"

"No, thank you very much, not just yet," Bobby says, surprising himself. The salesman nods graciously and Bobby leaves the store.

That evening, Lisa and Bobby search for famous Napoli pizza. After consulting the receptionist at their hotel, they choose a small bistro.

"We must remember this moment for the rest of our lives," Bobby says, raising his wineglass and looking around at the lively neighborhood. "We are about to eat pizza in Naples, where it was invented. Every pizza we eat from now on will be compared to this one."

Lisa laughs and raises her glass too. "To pizza in Napoli!"

At that moment, their waiter swoops over and places the large pizza they've ordered between them. After making sure they have all they need, he nods and disappears. They are surrounded by tables full of diners talking and laughing in the warm evening air. They each cut the pizza and begin to eat.

"Mmm, this is the freshest pizza I've ever eaten," Lisa says. "The tomato sauce is . . . so rich with flavor.

"Pizza began as poor peoples' food," Bobby says. "At first it was simply a flatbread, but eventually tomatoes and oil were added. The story goes that in the nineteenth century, a chef named Raffaele Esposito created the margherita pizza to honor Italian queen consort Margherita."

"So, Raffaele invented pizza as we know it?" Lisa asks.

"That's the legend. He added cheese and other toppings . . . and the rest is history."

Lisa watches a waiter pass with two dessert dishes with *sfogliatelle* filled with ricotta cream. "Did you see that?" she whispers loudly.

"We have to try it!" they both say at the same time, then burst out laughing.

Later that night at the hotel, Bobby and Lisa pack their bags. They plan to drive down the coast along the Gulf of Naples in the morning.

Shorts, white socks, flip-flops . . . Bobby reviews his wardrobe. *Maybe I should just buy an Italian shirt*, he thinks. *That would be a start.* Suddenly, he decides he will do it—and surprise Lisa with his newfound taste. *But what about a suit?*

When Lisa isn't looking, he researches a bit on his iPad. The luxury brand Brioni was founded in 1945 in Rome by a tailor and a businessman. Another brand, Cucinelli, is worn by Amazon founder Jeff Bezos. Though he was born into a family of farmers, Brunello Cucinelli is a billionaire today.

"I have to run out and do something," Bobby whispers into Lisa's ear the next morning. She stirs and looks at him quizzically. "I will tell you later. I won't be long."

He dashes out of the hotel and down the street, walking fast. No need for a map—he knows exactly where he is going. It's a crisp, sunny morning. He sees the store up ahead and is relieved to find it is open.

When he pushes open the door, the older salesman he'd seen the day before is right there, wearing the same fine wool suit, as if he'd never left.

"I want . . . I want to buy a shirt," Bobby says, slightly out of breath. "Maybe two."

"Of course, come see our selection," the salesman says, smiling.

SORRENTO

The drive south from Naples sends them through long tunnels and around harrowing curves on the way to Sorrento. Lisa has to shut her eyes when Bobby handles the sharp turns. He quietly grips the wheel of another rented Alfa Romeo, brooding about the job he hopes to get back home.

Why haven't I heard yet? It can't be good. He keeps his thoughts to himself. He doesn't want to burden Lisa with his worries.

Then, at last . . . Sorrento appears.

Deep blue water stretches out far into the distance, and beautiful towns perch impossibly in the mountainsides. Sorrento is going to be an expensive few days—but, Bobby reasons to himself, it's their honeymoon, the best time in life to splurge.

He bursts out singing a song Dean Martin made famous.

"Ma non mi fuggir, non darmi più tormento, Torna a Sorrento non farmi morir."

"What does it mean?" Lisa asks, moved by the song.

"He is saying, 'Don't leave me, don't torment me anymore. Come back to Sorrento, don't let me die.'" Bobby glances at Lisa and sees tears filling her eyes. "I know, very romantic, isn't it?"

They find their tiny hotel and check in. Then they walk along the Corso Italia in the heart of Sorrento, listening to street musicians serenade tourists and residents, who mingle in an easygoing way. The couple buys some gelato, which they savor—*Now we know how to discern the authentic variety,* Bobby thinks—but when she glimpses the open sea, Lisa insists they return to the hotel to change into their swimsuits.

After a quick change, they easily find a small beach nearby and sit down in two blue and white striped canvas chairs. The warm sun, the blue sky, the clear seawater—it's all blissfully beautiful.

Lisa stretches out her legs from the chair and sighs. "This is paradise," she says, lazily watching a sailboat course across the sea. How long has it been since she's worn a bathing suit? Too long, she decides, wiggling her toes in the sand and admiring their pink polish. She's glad she got a pedicure before coming to Italy. Even on the beach, Italians are stylish—she sees women wearing swimsuits and cover-ups by famous designers everywhere.

Soothed by the sound of the lapping ocean, she dozes. Three small children play in the water, shrieking with delight. They run up to their parents sitting under a red umbrella, then back to the water, again and again.

Would she and Bobby have one, two, or three children? And how will they manage children with their work lives?

Suddenly, Lisa feels something cold on her cheek. She opens her eyes to see Bobby holding two chilled glasses.

"*Limoncello!*" he says happily, handing her the cool, refreshing drink. They clink glasses.

"Where does this heavenly drink come from?" Lisa asks.

"Capri, I think," Bobby says, sitting back down in his beach chair. He is wearing a baseball cap to protect his head from the bright sun. "One story has it that a woman who grew oranges and lemons teamed up with her grandson, who made lemon liqueur, and created limoncello. The lemons must be from the Amalfi Coast, or the limoncello is not authentic."

"Oh, I taste vodka," Lisa says. "Delicious!"

Relaxing on the canvas seats in their swimsuits and dark sunglasses, Lisa and Bobby discuss the pros and cons of a day trip to Capri, the tiny island with blue grottos. They wonder, would it be too full of tourists?

"Let's ask that man over there." Lisa nods to an older gentleman reading a newspaper nearby. He wears a jaunty straw hat, baggy white pants, and a billowing pale blue shirt.

"*Per favore*," Lisa begins. "Do you speak English? Could you tell us your opinion . . . should we visit Capri? Is it as beautiful as everyone says?"

"*Buongiorno, sì*, I do speak some English. I can practice with you!" he replies with a big smile and pulls his chair closer to the couple. "I am from Rome and have come here for many years. I would tell you—yes, yes, you must see Capri! It is very beautiful, just as people say. And then you must go to Sicily—very good food! And much to see, including beaches."

"Thank you—*grazie*," Bobby says. "This beach is . . . *bellissima*. The whole coast is magnificent."

"*Sì, sì,* Italy has more beautiful beaches than any other country—but it is my country and I have been to most of them in my life." He laughs.

Lisa and Bobby sit up and introduce themselves. With a tip of his hat, the man says his name is Gianluigi. He has a kindly expression on his deeply tanned face.

"Italians enjoy being in the fresh air. In fact, we live a lot of our lives outdoors," Gianluigi says. "I am retired from my business of furniture design, so I am on vacation *tutto il tempo*—all the time," he laughs. "Do you two have jobs? Careers?"

"I study psychology," Lisa says proudly.

"I am an architect . . ." Bobby says. He suddenly wishes he could tell this stranger all about the job he's hoping to get, how it will help him begin is marriage with real confidence. But he says nothing.

"You have probably already found our weather exceptionally comfortable," Gianluigi goes on. "Of course, every region has cold spells, weeks of rain, or sweltering heat in the summer. But for much of the year, Italy's weather is mild and pleasant."

"Yes, we have noticed—it's lovely," Lisa says. "It's so easy to be outside all the time, at the beach, in the parks . . ."

"Our parks, yes, they have many old trees—older than I am! Borghese Gardens in Rome, it is always crowded on weekends with families," Gianluigi says. "It is pleasant any time of year. Citizens of Rome, children and adults alike, take off their shoes and run around on the grass, play games, ride bikes, and, of course, buy a gelato. My family and I used to go every Sunday when I was a child. Sometimes we spent the whole day there."

"Please, tell us your favorite beaches. What are your recommendations?" Lisa asks.

"Otranto is a city in the heel of Italy's boot," he says. "It juts out into the sea and its beautiful beach is a curve of white sand and pale turquoise water, perfect for swimming or snorkeling. You know Sardinia? An island in the Mediterranean—many idyllic beaches there—Cala Goloritzé, for instance, on the west side of the island, and Spiaggia di Tuerredda to the south. It's far away from traffic, crowds, and the worries of work. I like to wade through the warm, shallow waters, feeling the sand on my feet."

Gianluigi stops talking for a moment, lost in happy memories.

Bobby and Lisa look at him expectantly.

"Of course, across the water from Venice, Lido Beach is a good place to plunge into the cool water and invigorate your spirits," the man continues. "If it is too crowded in the summer, which it usually is, you can always rent your own cabana."

"Oh, I wish we'd done that when we were there. We'll definitely go next time," Bobby says.

"Another very beautiful beach is the *Scala dei Turchi*, or Turkish Steps, in Sicily," Gianluigi says. "Huge white sea cliffs made of limestone and marl have eroded to create a natural wonder—steps that take you right down to the water's edge." He pauses, then says, "You know, we take all of August for vacations . . . more than Americans, am I correct?"

Bobby nods. "Most Americans don't even take the days off their employers give them."

Gianluigi smiles at the young American couple. He hopes they visit all these beaches—Italian treasures, each one. "Where are you headed next in your adventure?" he asks.

"Palermo," Lisa replies. "But first, I think we need to check out Capri."

"*Molto bene! Allora* . . . it is time for my afternoon nap," Gianluigi says. "I have enjoyed speaking with you, happy to practice my English. I hope your trip to Capri is very pleasant. And the beaches, well, it is good for your spirit to be near the water. *Arrivederci!*"

CAPRI

The next day, Lisa and Bobby eagerly wait to board the sleek white ferry to Capri, along with many other tourists.

"Okay, what do we need to know about *KA-pree* before we go there . . ." Bobby says, flipping through his guidebook. "'Capri is only four square miles in size,'" he reads.

"So small," Lisa chimes in, "and yet so famous!"

"And the Blue Grotto is actually a cave. When the sunlight shines through the cave in the water, it looks blue and shimmery," he summarizes as the line inches forward. "Capri has two harbors and two main towns, Anacapri and Capri Town." He pauses to skim the page. "Ha! Lisa, listen to this: Caesar Augustus lived on Capri and built roads, houses, and aqueducts on it. And then his successor, Tiberius, built his Villa Jovis there because he was afraid of being assassinated and figured killers couldn't get here. Still, he imported his bread because he was afraid locals might try to poison him."

Lisa listens with amusement. For some reason, Bobby's reading doesn't bother her now. She appreciates his desire to know history, to understand people and the past. *Maybe being married to a person is to love the same characteristics that bother me*, she muses.

"And Liz Taylor lived here, and the poet Pablo Neruda . . ." Lisa says as the line of tourists boards the ferry. Within minutes they are out on the water, cruising across the Tyrrhenian Sea. Bobby tucks his book away and the two stand on the deck, marveling at the brilliant scene as the wind whips at their faces.

In less than thirty minutes, they disembark onto Marina Grande on Capri Island. Small boats bob in the blue harbor and tourists fill the streets. Lisa and Bobby stare at the huge craggy rock formations that soar up right out of the water.

"What is that?" Bobby asks the family next to him, thinking they are American. But he immediately realizes they are Italian.

"*Faraglioni*," the teenage girl says, pointing to the rock formations. "That is the name of them, the big rocks—*faraglioni*," she explains in heavily accented English. "Three of them, you know, they have special names . . . Stella is the one connected to the land. The second one is called Faraglione di Mezzo. And that last one is Faraglione di Fuori—the main one, the big one." The girl looks at Bobby and Lisa to make sure they understand.

Lisa thanks the girl, who gives them a little wave. She walks off with her parents and two younger brothers, each of whom carries a beach towel, chair, and a gelato.

Excited to explore the island, Lisa and Bobby take a taxi to Capri Town—one of many that waited near the curb. To walk all the way up would deplete their energy too soon. The driver heads up the narrow road that hugs the side of the cliff. When they reach the top, Bobby is happy to see restaurants everywhere, but it is too early for lunch. The view below shows them just how small the island is.

He and Lisa begin to walk along Via Tragara, enthralled by the combination of flowering plants and trees, the sheer size of the rocks, and the far-reaching ocean vistas splashed with brilliant sunlight.

They walk and walk. Then they come upon steps that lead to the faraglioni. "I never knew Capri had such lush nature," Lisa comments. "I usually hear about it as a place where celebrities take luxury vacations."

"Walking is the key to finding the hidden—and the best—places," Bobby says.

"Look, this is called the Neruda Path," Lisa reads off a plaque on the side of the path. "He had to leave Chile because he denounced their president for repressing miners. He lived here in 1952."

"A perfect spot for a poet," Bobby says, gazing around him. "It's like so many places in Italy—it appeals to all the senses at once. The beauty is so big and sweeping that it takes my breath away."

"While Neruda was here, he wrote *The Captain's Verses*, and it won the Nobel Prize in Literature," Lisa continues. "So I guess his exile in Capri was a good experience!"

"I think it's time for lunch," Bobby says, looking down the path toward the faraglioni.

After a delicious meal of seafood pasta, they ride on a funicular back down the hill and find a boat to take them out to the Blue Grotto, or *Grotta Azzurra*. With a group of twelve other tourists, Lisa and Bobby face the wind and eagerly look out for the famous grotto.

"We are lucky today—not many other boats!" shouts one of the boat crew as their destination comes into view. The afternoon sun warms their faces as the boat begins to slow down. Everyone leans out to see. The sparkling water looks inviting.

"Because there are few boats, it is safe to jump in for a swim, if you like—but only for a few minutes," the captain says. He is a middle-aged man wearing a blue windbreaker and white shorts.

Bobby and Lisa have been waiting for just this moment—they purposely wore their swimsuits under their clothes and brought towels in their bags. Quickly, they pull off their shorts and shirts and clamber down the steps on the side of the boat, with a hand from a crew member.

First Bobby jumps in, then Lisa. After taking a few strokes, they tread water to take in the rock formations around them and the stunning turquoise water.

"Oh, my God, this is amazing!" Lisa cries out. Her body

relaxes in the cool water. She dives under Bobby, then pops out on his other side.

Bobby looks about. The sunlight, the warm water—and the love of his life nearby. Joy courses through him. And what about the job? His worry drifts away for the moment. It feels good to be alive. "Everything is . . . perfect," he says. He dives down, pushing his body through the water, then taking more strong strokes when he reaches the top. He grabs Lisa's hand. "I'm so glad you married me, and that we came *here* to celebrate."

Lisa kisses him. She too feels a sudden sense of freedom. Her irritation with Bobby always reading facts from his books, and his terrible lack of style—none of it matters.

"Time to come back!" the captain shouts. All the swimmers reluctantly climb back aboard, giddy and refreshed.

Thermal Springs

Late in the day, they board the ferry back to Sorrento, feeling tired yet completely refreshed. They agree that one day they will return to Capri to explore more of this idyllic place.

The next morning, Bobby pays the bill at the Sorrento hotel. He and Lisa will drive back to Naples, then catch a flight to Palermo, where they hope to meet their college friend Marco.

"I hope you had a good visit," the young woman at the reception desk says with a cheerful smile.

"Yes, we did, *grazie*. I only wish we could stay longer," Bobby says. "The swimming was so refreshing. The water is so clear."

"*Allora*, if you like that, next time you and your wife must go to one of Italy's thermal springs," the receptionist says. "We have some very beautiful, special springs."

"Oh, we can't afford a spa visit," Bobby says.

"No, Italy has many springs open to everyone—not just the wealthy. It is good for health!"

"*Grazie*. Thank you for telling me about it," Bobby says. He marvels how Italy seems to look after its citizens.

Mi scusi . . . Dear reader, it's Nina again. That young woman is right! I want to tell you, this spring water—it can heal a lot of health problems. That's what my parents told me, and I believe them.

My family and I, we used to go sit in hot springs in our village in the afternoon sometimes. Even our mamma would come and put her feet in the water. And there would be our neighbors, cousins, and friends from other villages. We kids would run around in the trees and play hide-and-seek. I was very good at finding hiding places. I remember my cousins calling out, "Nina! Nina, *dove sei?*" And we would step over the big stones and look for the perfect place to sit where the hot water bubbled up. Once we'd had our fun, we would go back home for supper.

When Lisa was a little girl and I lived with her family in America, she used to call out, *"Nonna, Nonna, dove sei?"* It reminded me of my own childhood. This is one of the mysteries life gives us—how we can be children and then parents and then grandparents, a repeating circle of life, of families. It is sad and beautiful all at once, eh?

Ah, but those hot waters bubbling from the ground! So relaxing, *era così rilassante!* It didn't cost us anything. I laugh when I hear about the money people pay to go to a spa where they sit in a hot pool. We had that luxury—for free! These springs are a gift from nature, God, whatever you want to call it. And they are meant for everyone.

Oh, but let the writer explain . . .

Italy's natural thermal springs are a pleasing sensory experience. But, as Nina says, the waters are not just for rich people. Thermal springs are all over the country; some have been incorporated into high-end spa resorts, but many are free to the public, like the Parco dei Mulini in Val d'Orcia, Tuscany.

The most famous waters? They're in Saturnia, also in Tuscany. There, white mists rise out of hot, shallow pools of luminous blue water, which are fed by Saturnia's hot springs. These pools have been enjoyed since the Etruscan and Roman eras. Surrounded by rocky paths and bushes, the springs Cascate del Mulino and Cascate del Gorello cascade down in waterfalls and into the pools—perfect to sit in and absorb the warmth and therapeutic minerals. Bathers can walk from one pool to another. Italians who want to luxuriate here for a few days stay in Terme di Saturnia Natural Spa and Golf Resort, close by.

High above, Lisa peers down from the airplane window on the flight from Naples to Palermo, catching sight of the curve of Italy's boot. She and Bobby are eager to see their friend Marco, who is living in Palermo with his grandmother.

Sicily—more than nine thousand square miles in size—has the Mediterranean Sea to the south and west, the Tyrrhenian Sea on the north, and the Ionian Sea to the east. The Strait of Messina separates Sicily from mainland Italy. The island's terrain features mountains, including the volcanic Mount Etna, at more than ten thousand feet high.

"It will be so fun to see Marco in his own country. Remember how he told us parts of Palermo feel like a Middle Eastern city? And I hope we can see Monte Pellegrino as we land—the famous promontory. And . . . I can't wait to be in a real person's home," Lisa gushes excitedly. "Do you think Marco's grandmother will make food for us?"

"That would be incredible. I hope so," Bobby says. A feeling stirs inside his chest that he's getting used to: He wishes they could spend six months here, a year, or longer.

Taste

FOOD THAT FEEDS THE SOUL

PALERMO, SICILY

Marco spots Lisa and Bobby as soon as they step into the airport terminal. He waves frantically and rushes toward them.

"*Benvenuto!*" he says, embracing them both. "Come, my nonna has been preparing dinner for you all day."

Bobby and Lisa share an excited look. Their tall, gangly college friend talks nonstop as he drives them to their hotel— although he wanted them to stay with him on this visit, Bobby and Lisa didn't want to impose—and he keeps talking as he accompanies them when they check in and find their room to change their clothes.

"By the way, I am now an engineer," he proudly announces. "I finally got my degree and have a job here in Palermo. I live with my grandmother now, but I plan to get my own place soon.

But she makes all my meals, so it is hard to give that up. There is nothing like the food our grandmothers make. How do you say it in American slang . . . soul food."

A few minutes later, Bobby emerges from the room dressed for dinner. "Bobby, where did you get that beautiful shirt?" Lisa exclaims. His crisp, white linen shirt with narrow blue stripes is of obvious quality.

"*Amico, stai benissimo!*" Marco says, nodding in approval.

"You'll be interested to know, Marco, that Italy and my new wife—they are both influencing me, in spite of myself. I bought this shirt in Naples a few days ago."

"Okay, *amico*, now let's get to my nonna Gina's. We can't be late for dinner!" They leave the hotel and climb into Marco's tiny car parked on the street.

"Her name is Gina?" Lisa says, regarding Marco intently. "My nonna's name was Nina. She died a few years ago, but I remember one time she told me about a boy she knew whose name was Gino. How strange!" Suddenly Lisa feels as though she already knows Marco's grandmother.

"I remember you have family here. I hope you will see them—they will be very angry if you don't," Marco says.

As Marco navigates the narrow streets, he tells his friends all they need to know about getting around the city. "There are four historical districts, and they fan out from Quattro Canti—four corners. That will help you orient yourselves."

Lisa sniffs quietly. Suddenly, she misses Nina very much and wishes she could see her grandmother. There is so much she wishes she could ask now. *What was her little farm like? What did she grow there? Why didn't I ask her more questions when she was alive?* she wonders.

Marco parks his car next to an old stone apartment building and jumps out to open the car doors for his friends. The sun has set, so the streetlights guide their way to a big door. Inside, they climb up a flight of steps. An elderly woman with white hair and dark brown eyes greets them warmly in the entrance. They follow her to the kitchen, where a pot of sauce cooks on the stove.

"Nonna, what are you making?" Marco smiles. "And . . . when will it be ready?"

"It's a ragù, so it has to take time," Gina replies. Marco stands almost a foot taller than she does. He introduces his friends to his petite grandmother.

"I start making food and suddenly family and friends show up at the door. What am I making, Marco? Your favorite— ravioli," she chuckles, as if to say, "Of course!" She glances at Bobby and Lisa, who inhale the wonderful aroma of the cooking sauce.

"And what is in this sauce, Nonna?" Marco asks.

"How many times have you watched me make this, Marco, and you still don't remember? Pork, made with a fennel spice, tomatoes . . ." Gina turns to their guests and says, "The ricotta is made from cow's milk—I know the farmer—and I add a bit of nutmeg. It is a pleasure to cook for my family. To see them enjoy the food, well, it is why I cook."

Using her wooden spoon, Gina tastes the sauce, adds a pinch of salt, then gathers the ingredients to make the pasta and the ricotta filling. Just then, the doorbell rings. "*Avanti!*" Gina calls out. An elderly gentleman with gray hair and a crinkly smile enters. He hugs Marco and Gina. Marco introduces him as Francisco, his great uncle. Francisco opens a bottle of wine he's brought and pours four glasses full.

"*Cin cin!*" they cheer as they all sip the wine, sitting at the kitchen table and watching Gina cook. Francisco, Marco explains, owns a small but profitable vineyard. Bobby and Lisa ask Francisco about the process, curious to learn what goes into creating the sublime drink. After a while, Gina announces the ravioli and sauce are ready, and they bring the dishes to the table and help themselves to the fragrant good. "This is going to be the best food you've ever tasted," Marco tells his friends.

"*Buon appetito!*" Gina says as everyone digs in.

After one bite, Lisa stops, puts down her fork, and closes her eyes reverently. "You're right, Marco. Gina, this is . . . delicious, amazing!"

"Everything I learned from my grandmother," Gina says. "I watched her cook since I was a little girl. She would taste her food often and make little adjustments. She let me taste it too, and I would tell her what I thought it needed. I learned a lot just from her wooden spoon."

"Every meal you make is very, very good, Gina," Francisco says appreciatively to his sister. "What we taste is Gina's years of experience cooking, and also the years of our mother's and our grandmother's cooking—all their mistakes and discoveries."

"We have had amazing food in Italy. In fact, not one bad meal. But this one? This is the very best," Bobby says.

"You are traveling, so I will tell you this. When you go to a *ristorante*," Gina says, "you look for three things. One is a small menu. This means the cook knows how to make those dishes. A long menu means there will be inferior food. Two, look for a menu that is handwritten—this means the cook is using ingredients that are fresh today. He or she is creating dishes just for that day; they will change tomorrow. And third, ignore the places with a long board standing out front that lists all the dishes. They are trying to bring in tourists, not people who live here. Follow my advice and you will never be sorry."

The young people nod respectfully.

"How are the vineyards doing this year?" Marco asks his great-uncle. To Bobby and Lisa, he explains, "Sicily has a very robust wine industry, though most people don't know about it. Francisco's grapes are nourished by the rich volcanic soil of Mount Etna. Wine has been made in the area of the volcano for many years, but recently it has become very popular."

"Long ago, wine from Mount Etna was used in blends with other wines," the older man adds, "but now it stands on its own. And this has been a good year. The summer has been very hot, but it is okay."

"It's like Nonna's cooking," Marco says with a smile. "Generations of experience go into cultivating a vineyard. The sun, the rain, the temperatures—there are many factors."

"Making wine seems incredibly complex," Bobby marvels.

"It is an art," Gina interjects. "Sicilians have been making wine for centuries, that's why it's so good. He won't say it himself, but Francisco is very smart—he learned everything from our father and grandfather. He works hard. His wine is among the best. We know how to do this, our family."

The table falls silent as everyone appreciates the food and wine.

"This is so good, I will remember this meal forever," Bobby says. Gina and Francisco smile.

"Thank you, Marco, for bringing us here," Lisa says solemnly to her friend. "These flavors, they all make me feel . . . happy!"

"As they should!" Gina says. Everyone laughs, and Francisco pours another round of wine. Together, they toast Gina.

"Marco, what should we know about Sicily—and Sicilians?" Bobby asks.

"Well, Sicily is a big island—we have Mount Etna, we have beaches, we have magnificent churches . . . and we have Monreale."

"What's that?" Lisa asks.

"It is a village on top of a hill, with a very big medieval church that King William II of Sicily built sometime in the twelfth century. It has monks' quarters, tombs of famous people, including William . . . but the main feature is its massive glass mosaics."

"Yes, you must see them," Gina agrees.

"Of course, Palermo has many famous paintings, but it's not all old art here. You should visit the Museum of Contemporary Art. But I would say, in Sicily," Marco continues proudly, "your sense of taste will be surprised by the many flavors here. Because we are surrounded by ocean, the seafood is excellent. Sardines, mussels—if you walk through the street markets, you will see it all. And Lisa, check out the spices—you should buy some to take home. Here the influences are Spanish, French, African, Greek—"

"Palermo has a tree that is one hundred years old," Francisco suddenly interrupts. "A ficus tree. It is in the botanical garden, one of the finest in the world."

"And do you know of the qanat?" Marco adds.

"The *what?*" Bobby asks.

"Qanat—Palermo has an underground water system of channels that were built in the twelfth century by Arabs. They brought water from the aquifer to citizens over a wide area. It is an incredible bit of engineering! You can walk through them now—some people call it the cathedral under the city." Marco's love for this city is evident as he speaks.

"Okay, we have to see the markets and the qanat first thing tomorrow," Lisa says to Bobby. She is already thinking of the recipes she wants to replicate when she gets home: *I can bring these flavors into my own kitchen, and the same good feeling of this night at Gina's table.*

"Marco, take your friends out to see Palermo now," Gina says, and Francisco nods in agreement. "The city looks so beautiful with all the lights at nighttime."

"Is it too late for you two?" Marco asks.

"No!" Bobby and Lisa reply in unison.

So, after thanking Gina and Francisco for the food and wine, the three young people head out. Marco leads them to Via Chiavettieri, where crowds of people fill the tables lined up on the sidewalk, enjoying the warm night air. "These places serve the best *cicchetti*—little snacks—you will see," he says. The friends stroll on. "And here you will see oratorios, little chapels with mosaics, magnificent paintings . . ."

"Oh, I remember a story," Lisa says. "The Oratorio di San Lorenzo had a painting by Caravaggio, but it was stolen in the sixties sometime."

"And never found," Marco adds. "There are many rumors about what happened to it. Some say it was ripped apart and fed to pigs."

"I'd rather believe the thief hung it in his living room and has been admiring it ever since," Bobby says. He notices nearly all Italian architecture is lit up at night, creating sharp shadows and an entirely different look than in daylight. The original architects could never have predicted these lights, but they would certainly appreciate the theatrical play off of the buildings' forms.

A brightly lit cathedral looms before them. "This . . . is the Cathedral of Palermo. And that is Santa Rosalia, the patron saint of Palermo," he says, pointing to a statue in front of the cathedral of Rosalia raising a crucifix in one hand.

"Oh!" Lisa exclaims. "Tell us about her."

"She is the saint to call upon for protection from disease. In 2020, citizens prayed to her for protection against COVID-19," Marco replies, staring at the statue with seriousness. "She lived as a hermit in a cave, where she died. The story goes that during the plague in the 1600s, she appeared to a hunter and told him where to find her bones and where she wanted him to relocate them in Palermo. He did as he was told, and ever since she has been our patron saint."

Bobby and Lisa silently stare at the statue, processing Marco's story.

"Ah, now I will treat you to a true *dolce siciliano*: cassata cake!" Marco leads them to a crowded pastry bar nearby.

"What's in it?" Bobby asks.

"Ricotta, chocolate chips, lemon juice, candied fruit . . ."

"Say no more . . . let's try it!" Bobby says. The three hurry on toward the pastry bar.

The Joy of Good Food

Yes, food . . . what can I say? If you have eaten in Italy before, you already know what I'm talking about. I see people now go through these lines—still in their cars!—and buy this fast food, pah! I don't even call that food. They don't know what real food is. Italians know our food is good, and by this I mean it feeds *lo spirito* as well as the body.

When I watch my granddaughter Lisa and her beloved Bobby taste the good food here in a *ristorante*, there in an *osteria*, and best of all, made by a woman like Gina—well, my heart fills with happiness.

Here's what I need to tell you: From grandparents to parents to children, again and again, all over the country, Italians show their young ones how to make food. Why? We want to make sure our descendants are nourished by the same foods that nourished our ancestors. I hope kids today can put down their phones and shut their computers long enough to appreciate this good food, and maybe learn how to make it themselves!

You see, when we eat in Italy, we share everything with friends and family. If you could look in the windows of our homes, you would see plates of food and bottles of wine, and hear a lot of talk, a lot of laughing. It's the same north to south, from Milan to Sicily.

And in Sicily—well, cooking and eating, it's like a religion. Eating together is when we catch up with the news, tell everyone what is wrong with the world and what would make it right, and of course, we like to give advice to each other, even to the cook.

But here's what you need to know: When the fish market is closed, restaurants that depend on fish recipes automatically change up their menus. For a cook to serve less-than-fresh seafood is simply unacceptable.

Fresh food is cause for celebration—in fact, a lot of celebrations. In Italy we have strawberry festivals, lentil festivals, and sausage festivals. There are festivals of beans and of pine nuts, trout, and even truffles. Did you know Perugia has a chocolate festival every year?

There is a big food event in Apulia where everybody—

everybody—helps make big amounts of tomato sauce. It's a lot of fun, but you know the whole purpose is to pass on the process of storing the sauce—so you can eat it all winter—down to the newest generation.

And I can say this: *amore* is the most important ingredient when you're cooking food for your family, your neighbors, or your friends.

Italian cooks, they don't rush things. They choose all the good ingredients, get the measurements—which are usually based on what they feel—and adjust. A little more salt, a little more pepper. Stir it again with my old wooden spoon and taste. Ah, a few more minutes on the stove . . . You see, this is why you can't write down the recipes. It all has to come from experience. If you know this food is for your family, your best friends, it has to be good!

Lisa takes a walk by herself one afternoon, just to wander the streets of Palermo and take in the sights and fragrances of the neighborhood. She peeks into one small restaurant which is seating what looks like an entire family for an early lunch.

She suddenly thinks about Anthony Bourdain, the late food adventurist, who visited neighborhood restaurants on the outskirts of Rome during an episode of his TV series *Parts Unknown*. She remembered how the camera captured friendly young Roman waiters casually chatting with diners as Bourdain was shown to a table in one cozy restaurant. He was served wine and a plate of fresh ravioli lightly drizzled with olive oil. The camera zoomed in on the food and Lisa remembers she began salivating as she watched Bourdain cut into the delicate ravioli and eat it slowly, forkful by forkful. Savoring each bite, he groaned with happiness.

She smiles now recalling how he asked a friend why this food was just so delicious. The man explained: The cooks know that on any given night, their own neighbors, friends, and family are likely to arrive there for dinner, so they must make the best food possible. They want the diners to be truly happy, so every dish must be very, very good.

This happy memory reminds Lisa of another: *Pasta Grannies*, the YouTube sensation featuring older Italian women—one of them was one hundred years old—preparing gnocchi, ravioli, crepes, and other delicious food, all by hand. Once Lisa heard about this she had to watch every episode. They were funny, charming and informative. Created by Vicky Bennison, a British author and culinary traveler, the show depicted women moving easily around their kitchens, preparing complex dishes without a written recipe in sight. More than one said cooking is like therapy, and there was no mistaking their pride in the finished dishes.

Lisa thinks, *These women, who endured rationing and food restrictions during World War II, have been marked for life by that war. They waste not one bit of food in preparing family meals. And they love nothing more than to feed big groups of people, spreading happiness and a joy of living that they do not take for granted.*

"Do Italians still go to church?" Bobby asks Marco, who is leading them on their nighttime sightseeing walk through Palermo. They can't get enough of walking in Italy.

"No, not like they used to," Marco replies. "But no one misses the Sunday lunch! That is a long event—it takes hours," he laughs. "The family brings out their best dishes, the best wineglasses. Whole families gather when they can."

"Do the women do all the cooking?" Lisa asks.

"In the past they did, but now that so many women work outside the home, it's not always possible. It used to be that women would spend most of their days cooking."

"What happens to families without someone who cooks?" Bobby asks.

"Oh, no problem!" Marco says. "Restaurants and pastry shops are open on Sundays just for these people. And once the meal is over, everyone strolls the streets, searching for good gelato." He gestures to a nearby shop, attracting a line of these such walkers. "Do you know the phrase *fare la vasca*? It means essentially walking up and back, up and back, up and back, and this is what Italian people have done in their piazzas for centuries. And while they stroll, everybody checks out each other's clothing, and maybe they say hello or sit for an espresso."

"Ah, that's the real reason why Italians are so well-dressed." Lisa smiles. "They want to look good for their neighbors and friends who are observing them on Sundays."

Marco disagrees and shakes his head. "I think style is in the Italian blood."

Aperitivo, Cicchetti, and More

After saying goodnight to Marco, Bobby and Lisa walk back to their hotel.

"I like how Italians eat," Lisa says, spying their hotel up ahead. She looks forward to a good night's sleep. "Portions are modest, but no food is off limits. Instead of fixating on diets, they just eat really, really good food, which satisfies them."

"*Really* good food," Bobby emphasizes. "I've never eaten food like this before. The bar has been raised permanently. Even their little snacks are impeccably good. Haven't you noticed how in the hours after work and before dinner, people are out for a drink and a bite?"

"Yes! Crostini with anchovies on top, mini meatballs with breadcrumbs, artichoke hearts marinated with lemon and wine—isn't it called *aperitivo*?"

"I read that each region of Italy has *aperitivo* specialties people enjoy together in bars or outdoor tables . . . along with a cigarette!"

"Yes, and *cicchetti*, or small bites of food served in bars and restaurants, are like a kind of preamble to a full dinner. But I could eat *cicchetti* as a full meal," Lisa laughs. "Bread slices with ham and caramelized onions? Sausage meatballs with smoked cheese? Yummy!"

"Think of all the Italian words everyone knows that are food-related," Bobby says. "Al dente, ragù, cannoli, zabaglione, Bolognese, prosciutto, biscotti, spaghetti, calamari, marinara—these are famous! It just shows you how universally loved Italian food is."

The air is warm, and though it is late, restaurants are still open, light spilling from their doorways. Inside, Bobby and Lisa see tables full of diners.

"Compared to Americans, Italians eat slowly because everything is so tasty, so interesting. They don't want to rush through it." Bobby stops. "Lisa . . ." He leans down to kiss her. "I love you."

Lisa blushes and laughs. "Ah, it's the food," she says. "It's made you happy."

"Yes, I *am* happy," Bobby says, looking at her meaningfully. "Happy I married you."

Lisa smiles. Bobby looks quite handsome in his fine Italian shirt. Then she glances down at his worn running shoes. *It's a work in progress*, she thinks.

Smell

FRAGRANCES OF *LA DOLCE VITA*

TAORMINA, SICILY

"Mmm, *formaggio—un buon profumo!*" Lisa swoons.

She stands before a display of cheeses at a street market in Taormina, just off the main street, Corso Umberto I.

The day before, Bobby and Lisa said their goodbyes to Marco and his grandmother, promising to stay in touch and visit again as soon as they could. Then they rented a car and drove across Sicily to Taormina, a city of just ten thousand residents, situated between the Ionian Sea and Mount Etna on the island's eastern coast.

Now Bobby takes photos of fruits and vegetables in the market, most of which is shaded from the hot Sicilian sun by huge umbrellas. He has thrown a navy blue cashmere sweater over his shoulders—a *very* Italian look, according to Lisa. She bought it for him in Palermo.

One part of the market is inside a cool, open warehouse structure, and today it is jammed with vendors selling all kinds of food, like these cheeses Lisa is poring over. A heavyset man wearing a white apron behind the counter nods and says, "You like *formaggio*? Let me know if I may help you. I will do my best . . . my English is not so good."

"Can you tell me about these?" Lisa points to the display.

"Caciocavallo, mozzarella, pecorino, scamorza, ricotta, provolone . . ." the vendor says. "Good, made in Sicily."

Lisa studies the labels that explain how long each cheese has aged. "Asiago d'Allevo, *mezzano*, aged four to six months. *Vecchio*, aged ten months or longer. *Stravecchio*, fifteen months or more," she reads aloud. She wants to buy one, but they all look and smell so good. "How about that one, is it a Gorgonzola?" She gestures to part of a round of hard cheese wrapped in foil and cut open so the marbles of blue ripening fungus are visible.

"That one is more . . ." The vendor searches for the English word, but gives up. "*Intenso*," he says. "In addition, we have Gorgonzola *cremoso*." He points to a buttery-looking version that makes Lisa salivate.

"*Sì, capisco*." She nods, then spies another intriguing cheese. "Let me see one more, please. What is that one?"

"Grana Padano," he says proudly. "*Formaggio stagionato*, a hard cheese. We sell this at different stages of ripening. The older it is, the more *complesso*."

Lisa loves the look of all of them, but she wants to try a really local cheese. "Can you suggest one for a picnic today, to eat with bread and dried fruit?"

"Ricotta di Pecora, of course!" He smiles, offering her a piece to taste. "Sicilian ricotta is the best in the world. This one is soft, good with bread or nuts, or even chocolate."

"I'll take it!" Lisa decides. Once he wraps the large piece of ricotta in loose paper, she looks for Bobby, eager to tell him what is for lunch.

But Bobby is not easy to track down. He has wandered across the street to *il banco*, a counter in a tiny bistro where he's just ordered a coffee. He is shoulder to shoulder with other patrons, who quietly sip espresso from tiny cups—he is observing them discreetly.

"What are you doing?" Lisa asks.

"Shhh, I'm trying to be Italian," Bobby says. "First they ask for a glass of water, and when they get the coffee, they smell it before they drink it."

"One of the most heavenly aromas in the world—especially in the morning."

"Ah, here it is. *Grazie*," Bobby says to the barista who hands him a miniature cup. He looks down at the swirl of dark and light colors, then inhales the coffee deeply. He takes a sip. "Mmm, this is good."

Lisa is still intrigued by the tiny espresso cups. But people are drinking cappuccino in larger cups too. The aroma of strong coffee fills the air. "Caffè, latte, cappuccino—wonderful Italian words," she muses.

"Cappuccino is named after the color of the robes worn by Capuchin monks," Bobby says. "And coffee is so important in Italy. The beans, roasting, grinding, and the machinery and timing of each process—you can learn it all at a coffee university program here."

Where does he learn all this? she wonders. Then she remembers how much he reads.

"Ciao," say the two men standing next to Bobby, nodding to him and Lisa as they turn to leave. "Enjoy your Italian adventure!"

"What were you talking about with those guys?" she asks.

"Cars. Fiat, Ferrari, Lamborghini, Alfa Romeo—sleek, efficient, and fast—and all Italian. They told me about this event called Mille Miglia, or 1,000 Miles, which takes place in May. It begins in Brescia, in Lombardy. Drivers of vintage cars travel for days throughout some of the most picturesque towns in Italy. They recreate the original race, which was held for thirty years, from 1927 to 1957."

"Fun!" Lisa says. "I know nothing about cars, but I'd like to see that."

"Me too. Those two guys thought we would enjoy it."

"People seem to get friendlier the farther south we go," Lisa says.

"I know, it's amazing," Bobby says between sips. "They treat us like old friends, even though they seem to know right away we're American."

Aromas and Memory

For the afternoon in Taormina, Lisa and Bobby decide to seek out Villa Comunale, an elegant nineteenth-century home surrounded by acres of fragrant gardens with pathways, bridges, statues, terraces, well-placed stone benches, and arched bridges. It's another warm, sunny day. A salty ocean breeze ruffles the trees.

"Oh, this is luxurious!" Lisa says, taking a deep breath. "It smells so good here."

"Look, you can see the ocean, and way over there is Mount Etna." Bobby points into the distance.

"Aromas last longer in a person's memory than images do, don't you think?

"Maybe . . . yes," Bobby agrees. "I remember the smell of the ginger cookies my mother used to make at Christmas when I was little."

"That's what I mean! When I smell the incense in church services, it reminds me of my childhood. My nonna took me to church when my parents were busy. Incense makes the rituals all the more mysterious."

Lisa and Bobby sit on a stone bench to study the manicured hedges and meandering pathways before them, admiring the palm trees glistening in the bright midday sunlight. Lots of local people stroll through the gardens.

The villa and gardens were created by a British woman, but who was she, Lisa wonders. She is about to pull out her guidebook when a middle-aged Italian woman sits down next to her. The two nod politely, then Lisa says, "*Buongiorno*."

"American?" the woman asks with a friendly smile. She is clearly Italian, her English heavily accented. Her gray hair is stylishly cut and Lisa notes she is casually wearing a blue silk scarf around her neck.

"It is beautiful, yes?" The woman nods at the scene. "I am a teacher here in Taormina. I come here as often as I can for vistas like this." She turns to face them and says, "My name is Violetta. Are you on vacation?"

"We are on our honeymoon," Bobby says before he and Lisa introduce themselves. "You are very lucky to live here."

"Ah, honeymoon—*bella luna di miele!* Yes, I am lucky," Violetta says. "I heard you speak about the flowers a moment ago, the fragrances . . . I never take that for granted. This park is very special. It was designed by Lady Florence Trevelyan—she fled Britain because of a romantic liaison with Queen Victoria's son, Edward." Violetta smiles impishly. "That was lucky for us. She came here in 1884 to seek refuge, and look what she created. She was a fine gardener, as many British people are. She cared about birds and native plants and wanted to conserve them. She was forward-thinking, really."

"If I lived here, I would never need to go on vacation." Lisa gestures to the view.

Violetta laughs. "My husband and I go to Ischia. It's an island—have you heard of it? Flowers bloom year-round there. The wisteria and roses are so fragrant. The bougainvillea and birds-of-paradise are so colorful. You must go—it is like heaven."

"Is it true Maronti Beach on Ischia is one of the most beautiful in the world?" Bobby asks.

"Yes, it is . . . Italians go to Ischia to escape. Rich people go there to retreat, to forget about their troubles. My husband and I go for two weeks every spring. One of the prettiest hilltop villages is Sant'Angelo—we have a small house there. If you go, you will smell the sweet mixture of flowers and the sea."

"Didn't Richard Burton and Elizabeth Taylor have an affair in Ischia?" Lisa asks. "My mother used to mention it because she loved Richard Burton. She always said my father looked just like him."

"It's true—and it was a scandal!" Violetta says. Bobby now senses that Violetta enjoys spicy romantic stories. "They were both married to other people at the time. It was 1962 and they were filming *Cleopatra*. When they went out on a small boat alone together, well, the paparazzi captured it all. These photos still exist, I'm sure."

"Our generation might know Ischia from the books by Elena Ferrante, the series that begins with *My Brilliant Friend*," Lisa says.

Violetta nods, then gets up from the bench. "*Allora*, I need to get my exercise. I hope you enjoy your visit to Taormina—and this park."

"*Grazie*, it was a pleasure to talk with you," Bobby says.

Looking out across the ocean from their spot on the bench, Lisa takes another deep breath. *So many stories of romance, love,* she thinks. *No wonder so many people want to come here for their honeymoon . . . bella luna di miele.*

She is aware that she and Bobby are getting very close to the area where her grandparents had lived, and feels as if she is nearing a holy place that has influenced her life more than she ever realized. What will she find there?

"I'm practicing mindfulness," Lisa announces at dinner. It is their last night in Taormina. She sits back in her chair. "I want to take time to notice all the fragrances of this place—especially this meal right now." She closes her eyes and inhales the aromas of the food placed before her. "I smell garlic . . ." But she can't wait another second, and so she digs her fork into the pasta with breadcrumbs and sardines.

Bobby sips his red wine. "Did you know our sense of smell helps our sense of taste? And the way to release the aroma of wine before tasting is to swirl it."

"How do you do that?"

"Experts say you gently swirl a small amount of wine in a glass for about ten seconds to allow the aromas to vaporize into the air. And you're not supposed to deeply inhale, just hold the glass by the stem, lift it to just below your nose, and tilt it toward you at a slight angle."

Lisa follows these instructions, bringing her own glass to her nose.

"Now take a few gentle sniffs. You're allowed to open your mouth, so you can smell the fragrance through the nose and mouth at the same time," Bobby says.

She opens her mouth and breathes in. "*Mmmm.*"

"Now you're supposed to identify the aromas. Are they lemony? Fruity? Woody? Floral?"

"Oh, I don't know—I just want to drink it!" Lisa says. She downs the small amount of wine. "It's just good, that's what I know."

"Italy produces wine in twenty regions with a lot of different grapes, so this tasting and smelling, well, it's a lifetime practice," Bobby says. "One I hope to learn to perfect!"

He closes his eyes as he drinks from his own glass. When he opens them, he sees Lisa smiling from across the table. He picks up his fork to eat the delicate cooked fish on his plate, covered with tomatoes and olives.

As they eat, they both have the same thought: it's another wonderful night in Italy they will remember forever.

Just then, an elegant couple walks past their table, leaving in their wake the alluring scent of perfume. Both Lisa and Bobby turn to watch the couple glide through the restaurant.

Bobby remembers from his books that Italians have created alluring scents for centuries. He doesn't want to risk angering Lisa by talking about history, but once again he is filled with admiration for the Italian sense of business.

Italy manufactures some of the most popular fragrances in the world—many from regional ingredients, such as Sicilian oranges. In fact, the history of perfume in Italy began with a man named Renato Bianco, Bobby recalls. Renato was born around 1500 in Florence, abandoned as a baby, and raised by Dominican monks who grew herbs and made medicines. When young Renato grew up, he used this knowledge to invent his own chemistry to create scents.

Catherine de' Medici was just a teenager when she met Renato, who created a bergamot scent just for her. This perfume, still made today, is a top-seller called Acqua di Sicilia by Santa Maria Novella.

When Catherine married Henry II, the young queen took Renato with her to France, and his fragrances became popular among her friends there. He changed his name to René Le Florentin and opened his own perfume-making studio in Paris. So good at chemistry was he that Catherine is rumored to have put his talents to other uses—such as creating the poisoned gloves that killed Catherine's nemesis, Jeanne d'Albret, the queen of Navarre.

Bobby sighs, remembering these facts, and decides to buy Lisa a small bottle of Italian fragrance to surprise her later.

Orange Blossoms and Roses

"Bobby, did I ever tell you that when my nonna needed to think something over, she would walk in our garden?" Lisa says, getting out of their rental car.

They have arrived in San Giuliano to see the estate of the marquis, south of Taormina. As they approach, they smell the intoxicating scent of sweet citrus wafting from its garden groves.

"I always wondered why, but now I understand . . . gardens

are such a peaceful refuge. That's why I wanted us to visit so many of them in Italy."

"I hope one day we have a garden of our own," Bobby says, and Lisa smiles at him.

"You know, she also taught me to pick blueberries—*very carefully!* She promised that if I picked a lot of berries, she would make jam. It took so long, but I did it. Thinking about her jam now makes me happy. Ohhh, it is hot, hot, hot here!" Lisa fans herself with a guidebook as they approach the entrance. "Does someone actually live in this beautiful place?"

"The family still lives here. They produce and sell their own marmalade. Marmalade from Sicilian orange trees—who wouldn't want that?" Bobby asks, making a note to buy some on their way out. But first, they want to explore. They put on their hats and sunglasses, slather sunscreen on their arms, and walk along the sandy pathways surrounded by succulents and cacti.

As they wander the simple but elegant villa, they learn that the marquis and his wife, Fiamma Ferragamo, hired landscape designer Oliva di Collobiano—whose style trademark is blurring the boundaries between formal gardens and free-flowing nature—in 1990 to create a plan for their extensive gardens. Knowing the alluring power of fragrance, she made a scented garden, featuring licorice plants, myrtle, helichrysum, and citrus, as one of the four separate garden spaces on the estate.

Dear reader, Italians love flowers so much, we have a word— *infiorata*—that means "flower festivals"!

During these festivals, artists use colorful flower petals to make . . . what is the word? *Mosaico.* They are spread out over whole streets during spring festivals.

The most famous *infiorata*? I am proud to tell you it is in Sicily—Noto—where the flower designs cover the Via Nicolaci, a street of elegant palaces.

But all year round, we grow flowers in gardens that are peaceful places, where the fragrances and colors all come together—*molto tranquillo!*

Ah, listen, the writer wants to tell you something . . .

The *Grandi Giardini Italiani,* or great Italian gardens, is a network of 124 prestigious Italian gardens, coordinated by British entrepreneur Judith Wade. Dedicated to promoting horticulture tourism in Italy, she created this network to make sure these gardens could be identified and supported for future generations.

Old and extensive, many Italian gardens are prohibitively expensive to maintain. To offset the expense, some require tickets to visit or advance reservations for a guided tour. "[Italian] gardens are . . . proving increasingly popular with tourists looking for beautiful places to explore and relax in," Wade said in an interview.

Italian gardens are full of artistic surprises, such as topiaries— evergreens and shrubs pruned to grow in geometric shapes, or shapes of animals. Sculptures—of nymphs, gods, tyrants, and beasts—also pop up in Italian gardens, as do terraces, hedges grown in intricate patterns, water fountains, ponds, citrus trees in large terra cotta pots, and meandering pathways.

These gardens are "open-air museums that preserve hundreds of years of artistic and botanical history," says Judith Wade, author of *Italian Gardens*. Maintaining them is a national concern, she writes—Italians fear these old gardens will be lost in the country's expanding development. Some have been in the care of one family for generations, which often means there is no one left with the skill or money to keep the landscapes pruned, clipped, cleaned, and fertilized.

CATANIA, SICILY

From Taormina, Lisa and Bobby travel even further south to Catania, a large city on the east coast of Sicily, facing the Ionian Sea. Mount Etna looms in the near distance.

Lisa's cousin Lucia and her husband, Fabrizio, live about ten miles outside the city. They have invited Lisa and Bobby to stay with them for a few days—they hope to connect tomorrow.

As Lisa puts on her big straw hat that morning, she realizes she feels completely at home in Sicily. She's gotten used to the heat, the easy pace, the lack of pretention. Now, sunlight streams through their tall hotel room window. Bobby sits on the balcony, reading and watching the passersby below.

Lisa picks up clothes from the floor and wrinkles her nose. "I am washing your socks!" she declares. "I have smelled wonderful aromas in Italy—but not these socks!"

"All right, all right," Bobby says, thinking she is making a big deal out of nothing.

Lisa takes off her hat, brings their socks to their tiny bathroom sink, and washes them vigorously with soap and water. Then she looks around for a place to set them out to dry.

When Bobby glances up from his book, he sees her leaning out the window, carefully lining up the socks across the edge of the hotel façade.

"Be careful!" he says.

"All right, all right!" Lisa lovingly mocks him. Bobby laughs.

As the two head out for a walk, Lisa is glad for her hat, because the sun beats down on them as they wander the labyrinthine Catania streets. They stop at the Fontana dell'Elefante—a fountain with a sculpture of an elephant carrying a tall obelisk on its back.

Their walk quickly brings them to lunchtime. Alluring aromas of food drift through the air.

Bobby halts. "I smell fish!" he says. Then they see them: lunch diners at outdoor tables enjoying pasta with seafood—and not ten feet away is an open-air fish market.

"I guess there's no question. The seafood is fresh!" Lisa says.

Soon they sit at a table of their own, where they place their order with an attentive waiter. They each have a glass of sparkling white wine and smile broadly when their seafood dishes are placed before them.

As Lisa picks up her fork, Bobby teases, "Wait! Don't forget to be mindful of how the pasta smells."

Lisa laughs and inhales. "I smell tomatoes, garlic, fish . . . Let's eat!"

"I have an idea," Bobby says between bites. "Let's rent bikes after lunch and explore that way. I'm a little tired of walking and I saw a bike rental place around the corner."

"Okay, but I'm not very coordinated on a bike . . ." Lisa says, thinking, *It's been so long; do I even remember how to stay upright on a bike?*

With a little encouragement from Bobby, they buy bottled water after lunch and then find the bike rental shop. To her relief, Lisa takes to the bike much easier than she expected, and they enjoy navigating the streets a little faster than their usual walking speed. They cycle at an easy pace up one street and down another, following a narrow road that leads to the outskirts of town.

The afternoon wanes and sunlight throws a golden glow over the buildings and treetops. Bobby and Lisa take a rest next to an old stone wall. The sun is still hot, and insects buzz around them.

"I like it here," Lisa says. "Catania is a big city, but it feels comfortable, not overwhelming. And Mount Etna is so . . . grand. It's like a god looking over the city."

"Mount Etna has caused damage here," Bobby says, looking at the volcano warily. "More than once. Parts of it erupted just this year."

Giving in to their exhaustion after a long day exploring,

they get back on their bikes and pedal over the cobblestone streets. Suddenly, a big orange cat darts out of an alley right in front of Lisa's bike. She swerves to avoid it, loses her balance, and tumbles onto the sidewalk.

"Oooowww!"

"Lisa!" Bobby jumps off his bike and runs to her. A woman passing by runs to help Lisa too. She begins asking rapid-fire questions in Italian that Bobby cannot understand.

"I think I'm okay," Lisa says, sitting up, but she has a deep bleeding gash on her forehead.

"I'm not so sure," he says, trying to be calm. "We have to get you to a doctor." He turns to the woman. "*Dov'è un . . . dottore?*" he asks. The woman pulls a cell phone from her purse and makes a call, speaking so fast that Bobby cannot understand a word.

"*Tua ragazza?*" she asks him. "Your girlfriend?"

"No—she's my wife!" Bobby says, feeling fiercely protective.

Within a few minutes, a small ambulance speeds around the corner. A medic rushes to Lisa and asks what happened in Italian—then again in English when he realizes they are American.

"It is not dangerous, but I think the young lady must go to the hospital," the medic says to Bobby. "We need to check her." Bobby agrees readily. The woman offers to return their bikes to the shop, and Bobby climbs into the ambulance to be with Lisa, who has turned pale.

Is she all right? Bobby panics, his heart beating fast. *Nothing can happen to her.*

"I hear my American cousin had a dramatic fall in Catania!" Lucia says, entering the hospital room with her husband, Fabrizio.

"Lucia! You look exactly the same as when we were kids!" Lisa says. She sits up in the bed, her face now full of color. A large bandage is attached to her forehead. Bobby, staring at them both, sees an obvious resemblance between them—the dark red hair, large brown eyes, and easy smile. They could be sisters.

"And you . . . well, you look different," Lucia says, gesturing to Lisa's bandage, laughing. "Your husband called and told us you had an accident. What happened, my cousin?"

"I almost hit a cat in the street! I swerved to avoid it and I fell off my bike."

"*Mamma mia!* Don't worry about Sicilian cats," Fabrizio laughs. "They know how to survive."

Lisa introduces Bobby to her cousins. He shakes their hands warmly and Lucia opens a box of cookies she has brought for them to all share. They each take one.

"When you finish your cookie, dear Lisa, Fabrizio will bring you to our house to stay and recover. I will make you a good dinner and you will be better overnight!"

"It's true, Lucia's food makes everyone healthy," Fabrizio says. Lisa remembers Lucia and Fabrizio are also recently married.

"Fabrizio, it's so nice to meet you. Lucia has told me you work at home, but what do you do?" Lisa asks.

"I am an architect—I work out of the barn next to our

house. As you probably know, Lucia has a small organic farm. She grows oranges, lemons, and many legumes. People pay to come work with her to learn about organic farming. For us, it has been a very good year—I am busy, sometimes too busy."

"Wait, you're an architect? Bobby is too!" Lisa says. The men look at each other in surprise.

"Very good! I need a partner," Fabrizio says. "Maybe you can move here and we can work together." Bobby sees Fabrizio is only half teasing.

"I will consider that." Bobby feels a flush of excitement. "Thank you for coming to the hospital so quickly. I didn't know what we would do."

"Our house is very close," Lucia says. "And Lisa, our Nonna Nina and Nonno Lorenzo lived there, did you know this? You and Bobby will stay in her room."

Lisa's eyes grow big. "Nonna Nina, she lived there? With Lorenzo, with the red hair?"

"*Sì, sì!* She made the house and gardens beautiful, but after Lorenzo died she didn't want to be there anymore, so off she went to America to live with *tua madre* and your family. My parents and I visited you in America that one time, remember?"

"Yes, it was so long ago. I think I was six. It's so good to see you, Lucia! I am ready to get out of here right now—I want to see your home, Nina's home," she says. "I don't want to be in this hospital room another minute!"

"Lisa, the doctor has to see you first," Bobby says.

"Well, can you tell him to come see me right now? I want to see Nonna's house!"

"Okay, okay," Lucia says. "There is no rush. The house will be there. It is not going anywhere."

Bobby goes to find the doctor and soon Lisa is released into the care of her husband and family. Within minutes, they turn down a long, narrow driveway toward an old stone cottage, surrounded by flower gardens. Lisa looks out the window with tears in her eyes. This is the land her beloved Nina knew so well, a land of orange trees, olive trees, and grassy meadows. Lisa rolls down the car window and takes a deep breath of the warm, fragrant Sicilian air.

She feels like she's come home.

Dear reader, how it warms my heart to see these young people, *mia cara famiglia*! Look, there they are together in the house I loved so much, the house I lived in before I went to America. I am watching as they get to know each other and share stories of their lives. I am keeping watch over them, of course. I see Lisa is eagerly exploring the rooms of my former home and walking in the gardens I once tended. The bandage is still on her forehead—I laugh when I think she is so interested in resilience, when I see she herself has this very quality. Maybe she got it from me? She is a smart girl, my granddaughter—she pays attention and listens to people. I believe her intuition will serve her well.

Knowing
ITALIAN INTUITION

ROME

"Lucia and Fabrizio have such a wonderful life," Lisa reflects. "She reminded me of my nonna. Something about her easy-going outlook." Lisa is still flushed with happiness and gratitude that she reconnected with Lucia and stayed in her home—where Nina had lived for so many years. And just as Fabrizio predicted, Lucia's good cooking—meal after meal of homemade food—restored Lisa to health.

"Yes, I enjoyed them very much. They were so welcoming," Bobby says. He had also been delighted by Lucia's cooking.

The two are waiting in line to tour the Colosseum in Rome. After five days at Lucia's home outside Catania, Lisa and Bobby returned to Rome by plane. From here they will return to the US.

But for now, it's painfully obvious that they've only scratched the surface of all there is to see and do in this magnificent city.

Bobby cranes his neck to take in the full magnitude of the grand arena. He is in awe. *It's solid and elegant, and it's endured for centuries*, he thinks. "It's so much bigger than I realized." The line moves ahead and suddenly they enter the Colosseum's shadowy underside. "We must walk the whole circumference—it's about sixteen hundred feet . . ."

Lisa walks next to him, but her mind is on another track. "Gina and Francisco were welcoming too, as if we were family," she says. "There's just something about being around Italians. It's really comforting to me."

Bobby nods in agreement, but he is transfixed by the view above their heads. "Wow, can you imagine being here a few thousand years ago, watching gladiators fight?"

"No! I would hate to see that."

"It used to hold mock naval battles," an American man explains to his teenage son right next to Lisa. "The bottom part of the Colosseum was sealed and filled with water, on order from Emperor Titus. And then boats set out on the water and men put on battles—crazy!"

"Not crazy, Dad. It was like . . . their Super Bowl," the boy says.

"I guess it's another example of engineering ingenuity," Lisa says to Bobby with a laugh. "Let's keep going. I want to see it all."

After walking the perimeter, they climb to a higher level and walk around the arena again. A while later they sit and watch the sunlight shift. Lisa sighs. "Do we have time to get to the Capitoline Museums?"

"I think it's open for another hour. What do you want to see?"

"Constantine," Lisa replies. "He converted to Christianity, though I'm not sure his intentions were good. He might have just wanted more power. They have a big sculpture of him there."

They quickly head over to the museum and find it empty of visitors. Lisa rushes toward the massive bronze head of Constantine, the ruler of the Roman Empire, which sits in an open, airy room. Bobby takes a photo of her standing next to the gigantic head, whose huge eyes stare into the distance.

"I'm going to ask the guard if the famous bronze she-wolf statue is here. It's the one meant to represent Rome," Bobby says. As he disappears into another gallery, Lisa is drawn to a display of plates.

After a few moments, she looks up but doesn't see Bobby anywhere. She walks into the next room of the museum, but he's not there. Then she turns back to look into another room by the entrance—he's not there either. She asks the guard where the she-wolf statue can be found, and is disappointed that Bobby is not in its gallery room.

She turns around and around. *Where could he have gone?* She pulls out her phone to text him, but her phone has gone dead.

She walks back to the entrance to find another guard. "*Per favore . . .*" she begins.

"Let's walk to Trastevere—it's supposed to be a fun neighborhood, full of great places to eat," a voice says behind her.

Lisa spins around—Bobby is right next to her. "Where were you?" she asks.

"Right here," he says. "In that little room—amazing Roman artifacts."

Lisa grabs his arm. "I lost you for a few minutes." *I don't ever want to lose you*, she thinks, pulling herself close to him as they head out to find dinner.

The streets narrow when they enter Trastevere. Waiters set candles on outdoor tables, and Lisa hears the pop of wine bottles uncorking. She and Bobby approach an eatery and are soon seated at a table of their own. They order, then sit back to enjoy the scene.

"When we left Gina's house, she squeezed my hand in this very kind way," Bobby says. "It was as if she knew everything about me and forgave me all my faults." He laughs and shakes his head, not understanding how that could be.

"I've noticed that in the eyes of a lot of Italians," Lisa says, "especially the older ones. It's like they've seen it all. Nothing surprises them."

A family of four passes their table, looking for a place to sit. Their two little boys are having boisterous fun while their parents help them into their chairs.

Bobby glances, then does a double-take. "It can't be . . ." he says, getting up from his chair. Lisa follows his gaze, confused. "Isabella!" Bobby calls out, and the mother of the family turns her head and breaks into a broad smile.

"Bobby!" she shouts, instantly recognizing her long-lost high school friend from her time in America.

The two groups push their tables together with the waiter's help. Bobby introduces Lisa, then Isabella her husband and their boys.

"How many years has it been? So many! Do you live here in Rome?" Bobby asks.

"*Sì*, I have lived here since high school. Remember, my family left the US right after graduation? My father's family is from Rome and he wanted us all to return. I met my husband, Mario, soon after that." Mario beams from his seat, then he orders several bottles of wine for the table.

"Lisa, it's very good to meet you," Isabella says. Her long, dark hair is held back in a thick pony tail. She wears little makeup, but her face is vibrant and happy. She explains that she is a teacher and her husband is a doctor. "When Bobby and I were teenagers, he was the only one who loved the opera music I played at my parents' house. Of all the kids in our group, he was the only one interested that my family was from Italy. I knew he would come here one day."

"Opera, yes, we saw *Aida* at the Arena di Verona. It was fantastic!" Lisa says. She is excited to meet someone who knew her husband so long ago. "I'm just learning about opera, but I do like it."

"If you like opera, there is much for you to hear in Italy," Isabella says. While Bobby and Mario talk on the other side of the table, Lisa wants to ask Isabella some questions for her psychology research. Isabella leans in with interest.

"Italians exude a confident understanding of people and life that translates into intuition," Lisa says. "Is this because they come from close-knit families where traditions are shared from grandparents to children?"

"*Sì, sì,*" Isabella says, thinking for a moment. The waiter pours wine into their glasses. "Families stay together, work together, eat together. For instance, recipes are committed to memory—cooks have a very good sense of ingredients and cooking times, of what's needed and what's missing. Italians who are in their seventies or older have lived through a lot—they have known real suffering. As a result, they guard their families, and they work together to survive. Keeping the family together, safe, and healthy is of utmost importance."

"I read that Sophia Loren once said, 'The two big advantages I had at birth were to have been born wise and to have been born in poverty,'" Lisa says. "I think she means wisdom and being poor can be connected—once you know what it's like to be hungry, you will never take food for granted."

Isabella agrees. "Not taking anything for granted is necessary for survival, whether you are living in calamity or peace. People who are determined to earn a living can live with less, if they have to—they are the ones who will survive."

Isabella's two boys erupt in an argument and she turns to help them work it out. Their dispute is about whether Gianluigi Buffon or Giorgio Chiellini is a more valuable soccer player.

"Another thing, Lisa, our *nonne e nonni*—grandmothers and grandfathers—are dedicated to caring for their families . . ."

"It seems like a very good way to live," Lisa says. "If you are connected to a network of friends and family, you are protected emotionally—and physically too—far more than loners." She is quiet for a moment, thinking about her long-held wish to be part of an extended family.

Just then, the waiter delivers plates of food. The reunited friends eat and talk late into the evening, until the little boys start yawning. Isabella, Lisa, Mario, and Bobby exchange contact information, and after much hugging, they say goodbye.

Immigrants

Dear reader, it wasn't easy for me to come to America. It was *molto difficile*! Maybe it was not as hard as those who came before me—no, certainly not. But I had to learn a new language and understand a new culture in America when I came to live with Lisa and her parents. They welcomed me and cared for me lovingly, and I will always be grateful.

But that was not how it was for the Italians who came to New York City in the 1880s. You know, immigrants who arrived in America until the 1920s, they were determined to survive! They were hungry, sick, and treated very badly as they came to so many cities on the East Coast of the United States. All they wanted was a better life. The men, they worked dirty, dangerous jobs, building dams and digging tunnels for subway lines.

Thank God for the missionaries. Do you know of Mother

Cabrini? Sisters like her saved the poor Italians in America. What the sisters did—they got rich Italians to donate money—it was only right!

I was never rich in money . . . but I was rich in family, rich in good health. Yes! I was healthy right up to the last minute, dear reader. Let this be a lesson: You never know when it's all going to be over. And I was old—ninety-three!

You know, Italians live a long time. And we don't "retire" the way Americans do—we keep busy to the end. Have you seen Sophia Loren? She is still making movies—*mamma mia!* And she is still very beautiful. We Italians take care of ourselves, we eat well, we take our vacations . . . so we are healthy and live a long time.

Oh, here, the writer wants to share some stories with you about this.

Sophia Loren in her eighth decade starred in a new movie, *The Life Ahead*, produced by her son, Edoardo Ponti.

Gina Lollobrigida is in her nineties.

Giorgio Armani is in the second half of his eighties.

Vibrant, successful, stylish—these Italians have lived a long time and are icons of the good life. And with age naturally comes wisdom, having "seen it all."

But these are just the famous ones. Among European

countries, Italy has proportionally the most people over the age of eighty. And the number of Italians who are one hundred or older has tripled in the past fifteen years. Italians are social, outgoing, and surrounded by a family network that protects them as they age.

Emma Morano, for example, was the oldest living person in the world until her death in 2017 at age 117—and she is the longest-living Italian in recorded history. She was born on November 29, 1899, eight months after the Italian entrepreneur Guglielmo Marconi made the first radio transmissions across the English Channel. In Emma's lifetime, two world wars were fought, the airplane was invented, antibiotics were discovered, and computers became common household objects. She saw ninety Italian governments come and go.

Emma was unhappily married and had one child, who died as a baby. She later left her husband and started work in a jute factory and in a boarding school kitchen; she retired at age seventy-five. As she aged, people often questioned her about her longevity. She claimed it was due to her diet of eggs, chocolate, and grappa—and her positive attitude.

Emma died in 2017 at her home in Verbania on the shore of Lake Maggiore, northwest of Milan. Her lifespan is rare, but many Italians are living longer than ever before.

"Let's go this way . . ." Lisa says, pointing to a line on Bobby's map. They have wandered into a neighborhood on the outskirts of Rome and are completely lost.

"We actually need to go in the opposite direction." Bobby frowns. "See that church over there? We need to turn there to get back to the hotel."

"No, you're wrong . . . Look, we need to find this street, then that park. *Come on!*"

"Okay, bossy!" Bobby bursts.

"Me? *You're* bossy!" Lisa turns to walk in the direction she chose.

"Lisa!" Bobby says, his voice full of frustration.

In the distance, a middle-aged Italian man and woman sit on a bench in the shade of a nearby tree and watch with amusement as Lisa and Bobby argue.

Finally, Bobby looks around and sees the couple. He decides to approach. "*Per favore*, we're trying to find the metro station," he says.

"Two blocks in that direction," the man says in English. "But it will be very crowded. You might want to walk."

Lisa comes back and sits on the bench, arms folded, still angry. "I need to rest for a few minutes."

"*Sì, sì*, have a rest, drink some water," the woman says kindly, pointing to a public fountain a few feet away.

Lisa takes a deep breath and looks at the older couple.

"Are you here on vacation?" the woman asks.

"No, it's our . . . *bella luna di miele*," Lisa says.

"Ahhh!"

"Everyone has been so helpful to us here," Bobby says. He sits down and puts his arm around Lisa.

"*L'amore, matrimonio*, not easy . . ." The man smiles at

them. "There is disagreement, there are times with money, times without money . . . but *l'amore* is stronger than all the difficulties—it keeps you going. *L'amore* helps you get through the troubles. It creates a kind of . . . *resilienza*."

"Resilience!" Lisa says.

The man smiles. He and his wife get up slowly from the bench and wish Bobby and Lisa a good afternoon. "Ciao," they say in unison.

As Bobby and Lisa watch them walk away, they reach for each other's hands.

"I hope we are like that one day. Old and content."

"I think we will," Bobby says, squeezing Lisa's hand reassuringly. "Shall we go?" he asks, and Lisa nods. "You lead the way."

Pragmatism

GOOD SENSE

"Italians are down-to-earth people," Filippo tells the two young Americans, as if stating a known fact.

The rotund gentleman wearing a crisp white shirt has just seated himself next to Lisa and Bobby at their table at his restaurant near the Pantheon in Rome.

It's near closing time—the time Filippo enjoys getting to know lingering diners. He likes this young American couple. He senses their desire to understand Italy and Italians. He's wants very much to give them the correct insight.

"We have famous artists and musicians, but don't forget, we have many important scientists, philosophers, educators, engineers . . . Romans built an entire aqueduct system thousands of years ago. It transported water across hundreds of miles to the people who lived in cities."

"With no bulldozers!" Bobby marvels.

"No bulldozers!" Filippo says, bursting into a hearty laugh. "In fact, ancient Rome depended on eleven aqueducts." He turns serious. "The aqueducts were *molto forti*—some of them still stand today. The Fontana di Trevi is still fed by water from an aqueduct."

"That's incredible!" Lisa says. "So . . . pragmatic means thinking of what's good for everyone. I see that in the train system. The trains are clean, they are on time, and you can get anywhere in the country—or in Europe. *That* is pragmatic."

"*Sì, sì*, very true," Filippo says. "We take the trains for granted, but most Italians rely on them."

"When I think of pragmatic, I think of being smart at business," Bobby says. "You know this better than anyone—your chef creates fantastic food. But *you* keep track of the numbers, the profit. Without that, restaurants could not survive. And Italy is full of small, thriving businesses."

"*Sì*," Filippo agrees. He turns and gestures to the dozen tables where diners savor their wine and desserts. "That's why I employ my family. The chef is my oldest son—he learned to cook from my mother. The three waiters are my nephews. The hostess at the door, my niece. My wife and I, we keep the books. When the tables are full, it is good for all of us. *Molto pragmatico, sì?*"

Bobby and Lisa smile, and Filippo continues. "I started working at a young age—it gave me independence. Now I share my business with my family. Let me tell you, Italians welcome millions of visitors from around the world every year. Tourism is a big part of our economy—hotels, ski slopes, beach resorts, and thousands of restaurants like mine. We make visitors feel welcome by making sure the rooms are comfortable, the buildings safe, the streets clean, transportation easy . . . but for me, I enjoy it. This *ristorante* is more than a livelihood, *è la mia vita!*"

"We have certainly benefitted from it tonight. *Grazie*," Lisa says.

"Italy is an easy place to spend a lot of money—without regret!" Bobby adds.

"That is good," Filippo laughs. "We Italians disagree and argue, but we know how to work together. We want you to be happy and for us to be happy. How much longer will you be here?"

"We leave in two days," Lisa says sadly. "I could stay forever."

"Here, please, take my card. And when you return, you will come again. It's been a pleasure. And *buon viaggio*." Filippo rises, shakes their hands, and says, "Ciao!"

Lisa is uncharacteristically quiet as she and Bobby walk back to their hotel.

"What are you thinking?" Bobby asks.

"I know what my thesis topic is going to be," she says. "It's going to be about the resilience of Italian people—and I will focus on my nonna's generation, people born in the 1930s. They saw and survived so much! They are part of what makes Italy so great."

"That is a fantastic idea," Bobby says. "You've been taking notes about everyone we've met on this trip, haven't you?"

Lisa smiles. "Yes, I have."

The next morning, they decide to walk around Rome with no agenda but to soak in the sights and sounds before they leave.

On a busy commercial street, Bobby stops in front of a store window displaying sleek laptops and cell phones—white, black, and silver devices. He marvels once again at the ingenuity of Italian design.

"Do you know the name Olivetti?" he asks Lisa, who joins him at the window.

"Yes—didn't they make typewriters?"

"Not just any typewriter—the first portable typewriter, which was a huge hit, as you can imagine," Bobby says. "My father had one, and still has it. He always said Olivetti was ahead of his time. People were traveling, on the move, and Olivetti recognized a need for a portable typewriter. The idea of a typewriter so sleek and light that it could be taken from office to home—that was groundbreaking."

"Ohhh, Prada!" Lisa interrupts, stopping to admire a shop window filled with handbags. "Is there anything more Italian than Prada?"

"Pasta?" Bobby teases. "Okay, Lisa, if you must go into this store, I understand. In fact, I might need to buy some Prada sunglasses. I am trying to upgrade my look."

Thirty minutes later, Bobby and Lisa emerge from the store with big bags filled with their purchases. Bobby sighs, "That was a lot of money . . . but I don't regret it at all."

"Neither do I," Lisa says. "I am happy to contribute to the Italian economy!"

As they pass a bank, she says, "Did you know banking as a business was begun by the Medici family? So much that we take for granted started in Italy."

Dear reader, *per favore*, I want to tell you one more thing. When I decided to go to America, of course I lived the same way I always did.

But immigrants, once we decide what we have to do, we are *molto forti*, and one way to survive is to keep up traditions— and that includes our church and celebrating the feast days. I insisted Lisa go to a Catholic school when she was a little girl, so she would have a good education and a strong foundation with God. We immigrants, we want our children to be strong, of course, and to succeed. I hope I taught my children well, and I see that Lisa is a strong young woman.

Look, she married a smart professional, and she is going to be one herself—*una donna di successo!*

"Did you know . . . there were a lot of Italian *scientists?*"

It is the afternoon before their flight back to the US. Bobby had been packing one of his Italian history books when he stopped to read a few pages.

Lisa is trying to find room in her suitcase for all the purchases she made in nearly every city.

"Yes," she says, "Galileo, Alessandro Volta, Leonardo da Vinci, Enrico Fermi . . ."

"What about Maria Gaetana Agnesi—have you heard of her?" Bobby quizzes.

"No, who is she?"

"She was born in 1718 and was a mathematician, philosopher, and theologian. She was the first woman math professor at a university, and the first woman to write a book on the subject," Bobby says.

Lisa suddenly gasps. "Those *shoes!*" She points to the soft leather loafers on Bobby's feet. "Where—when—did you get them?"

"I thought you'd never notice!" Bobby laughs. "I got them yesterday on Via Condotti. Do you like them?" He stretches out his feet to show off the new shoes.

"They are fabulous," Lisa says. "I'm so proud of you . . . and look, your whole style is very Italian!" Bobby's dark curly hair has grown a little wild, and she finds it very attractive.

"Lisa, we have one more place to go—the Vatican. Are you ready?"

"Yes!" she answers, glad to abandon the packing.

They wind their way on foot through the streets of Rome. Saint Peter's Square is open and expansive. They stare at the wide double ring of columns, the crowds of late afternoon visitors—and the basilica at the end of it.

Bobby and Lisa are drawn to the commanding Egyptian obelisk at the center of the square. There they turn around and around, arms outstretched, taking in the full panoramic view.

"Rome! Italy! We are like pilgrims arriving at our final, most important destination," Bobby says.

"I feel like some presence has been guiding us all through Italy," Lisa says dreamily.

"I do too," Bobby says. Then he looks at his watch. "Let's go—our tickets for the Sistine Chapel and the Vatican galleries say we have to be there on time."

Inside the hushed chapel, they crane their necks to see the lifelike frescoes on the ceiling and walls. A guard reminds everyone this is a chapel, so no photos are allowed, and voices are to be kept low. Lisa grips Bobby's arm as she looks up at Michelangelo's fresco of God reaching out to touch Adam. She has seen reproductions of this image all her life, and it takes her breath away to see it in person.

"These people look like they are hovering right above us," Bobby whispers staring up. "Look over there—" He points to an image of figures in a boat while other figures cling to each other as if for dear life.

They move through the chapel to the exit.

"There are fifty-four Vatican galleries, filled with art, sculptures, and artifacts," Bobby says. "Let's see as many galleries as we can. Our reward will be dinner."

"Sounds like a plan!" Lisa says.

"I made a reservation somewhere your cousin Lucia recommended. In fact—I can't keep a secret—she gave me money to pay for this dinner as a honeymoon gift. She gave it to me on one condition—that we come back next year and stay with her for several weeks."

"Oh, how nice!" Lisa says, and her heart feels full. *I have family, real family, in Italy!*

Suddenly, Bobby's phone buzzes. "Who could be texting me?" He pulls out his phone and reads the incoming message. "It's . . . Oh, wow!"

"What is it?"

"I got the job—they're offering me a year's contract!"

Lisa claps and jumps up and down. "Congratulations! When do you start?"

"The week after we get home."

"Oh, my gosh, this is great!" She beams at him. "But I confess, when Fabrizio made that comment about needing a partner, I immediately fantasized about us moving there to live near them so that could happen . . ."

"I did too," Bobby says. "And we still could. I mean, this is a year's contract, which will help me get some good experience. Then after you get your degree, we can come back here and both work."

They look into each other's eyes and burst out laughing.

At the direction of the flight attendant, Bobby and Lisa fasten their seat belts. They are not ready to begin the long plane trip home from Italy.

"How do you feel?" Lisa asks.

"Exhausted, changed, happy, sad," Bobby says. "All my senses have been awakened and will not shut down. We've seen amazing art, and eaten food so good I almost cried. We walked through ancient arenas where gladiators fought, and we swam in clear, warm water on amazingly pretty beaches."

"Italy is so much more than I ever realized. Already, I miss everything. Italians seem to enjoy life more than any other people I've met." She pauses for a moment, reflecting on their perfect honeymoon. "Maybe the only way to keep this fresh in our minds is to plan our next visit."

"Well . . ."

"Or live here!" Lisa says. The two look at each other and laugh again. The idea is starting to sound more possible by the minute.

"Okay, but until then? Let's try to be as Italian as possible. I'm taking an Italian cooking class as soon as we get back."

"I'm going to take the next level of Italian language," Bobby says. "I bet there's an app I can get."

"I want to watch all the best Italian movies. *Roman Holiday*, all the Fellini movies . . ."

"And I want to read books by Italians or about Italy— Umberto Eco, Elena Ferrante, Donna Leon . . ."

"But, you know, the part of Italy that changed me the most was how Italians see the beauty in life, the positive, the good. They were so incredibly kind—Marco, Gina, Francisco, Isabella, Mario, Lucia, Fabrizio—they made us feel so welcome, like family."

"It was the perfect way to begin our life together," Bobby says, turning to look into Lisa's eyes. She squeezes his arm as the plane takes off.

So, you see, dear reader, I have been useful even after death, to push Lisa and Bobby to see the beauty of Italy. What a journey, eh? My heart goes with them. I think they learned a few things along the way, don't you?

Sono molto felice—I am very happy.

Now, my next wish: *per favore*, a few great-grandchildren?

About the Author

Nicole is a writer and editor living in Southern California with her husband and son. She has been the home and garden/travel editor at the *Orange County Register*, and has written and edited for numerous publications, including *VIV* magazine, *Family Circle, the Boston Globe, Los Angeles* magazine, the *Los Angeles Times*, and others. Recent features she's written include stories about a treehouse designer, why we need a surgeon general, how a cocoa bean chemical can reverse memory loss, and reasons to take an inn-to-inn hike along the Southern California coast. When she's not obsessing about her garden, she enjoys traveling, cooking, and reading fiction.

ALSO FROM THE MENTORIS PROJECT

America's Forgotten Founding Father
A Novel Based on the Life of Filippo Mazzei
by Rosanne Welch, PhD

A. P. Giannini—Il Banchiere di Tutti
di Francesca Valente

A. P. Giannini—The People's Banker
by Francesca Valente

The Architect Who Changed Our World
A Novel Based on the Life of Andrea Palladio
by Pamela Winfrey

At Last
A Novel Based on the Life of Harry Warren
by Stacia Raymond

A Boxing Trainer's Journey
A Novel Based on the Life of Angelo Dundee
by Jonathan Brown

Breaking Barriers
A Novel Based on the Life of Laura Bassi
by Jule Selbo

Building Heaven's Ceiling
A Novel Based on the Life of Filippo Brunelleschi
by Joe Cline

Building Wealth
From Shoeshine Boy to Real Estate Magnate
by Robert Barbera

Building Wealth 101
How to Make Your Money Work for You
by Robert Barbera

Character is What Counts
A Novel Based on the Life of Vince Lombardi
by Jonathan Brown

Christopher Columbus: His Life and Discoveries
by Mario Di Giovanni

Dark Labyrinth
A Novel Based on the Life of Galileo Galilei
by Peter David Myers

Defying Danger
A Novel Based on the Life of Father Matteo Ricci
by Nicole Gregory

Desert Missionary
A Novel Based on the Life of Father Eusebio Kino
by Nicole Gregory

The Divine Proportions of Luca Pacioli
A Novel Based on the Life of Luca Pacioli
by W. A.W. Parker

The Dream of Life
A Novel Based on the Life of Federico Fellini
by Kate Fuglei

Dreams of Discovery
A Novel Based on the Life of the Explorer John Cabot
by Jule Selbo

The Embrace of Hope
A Novel Based on the Life of Frank Capra
by Kate Fuglei

The Faithful
A Novel Based on the Life of Giuseppe Verdi
by Collin Mitchell

Fermi's Gifts
A Novel Based on the Life of Enrico Fermi
by Kate Fuglei

First Among Equals
A Novel Based on the Life of Cosimo de' Medici
by Francesco Massaccesi

The Flesh and the Spirit
A Novel Based on the Life of St. Augustine of Hippo
by Sharon Reiser and Ali A. Smith

God's Messenger
A Novel Based on the Life of Mother Frances X. Cabrini
by Nicole Gregory

Grace Notes
A Novel Based on the Life of Henry Mancini
by Stacia Raymond

Guido's Guiding Hand
A Novel Inspired by the Life of Guido d'Arezzo
by Kinglsey Day

Harvesting the American Dream
A Novel Based on the Life of Ernest Gallo
by Karen Richardson

Humble Servant of Truth
A Novel Based on the Life of Thomas Aquinas
by Margaret O'Reilly

Relentless Visionary: Alessandro Volta
by Michael Berick

Retire and Refire
Financial Strategies for All Ages to Navigate
Their Golden Years with Ease
by Robert Barbera

Ride Into the Sun
A Novel Based on the Life of Scipio Africanus
by Patric Verrone

Rita Levi-Montalcini
Pioneer & Ambassador of Science
by Francesca Valente

Saving the Republic
A Novel Based on the Life of Marcus Cicero
by Eric D. Martin

The Seven Senses of Italy
by Nicole Gregory

Sinner, Servant, Saint
A Novel Based on the Life of St. Francis of Assisi
by Margaret O'Reilly

For more information on these titles and
the Mentoris Project, please visit
www.mentorisproject.org

Made in the USA
Middletown, DE
05 February 2025

70231397R00130